Colin Dann was born in Richmond, Surrey. His interest in natural history was fostered by studying the local wildlife in Richmond Park, and wildlife success came at the age of ten, when he won a London Schools Essay Competition set by the RSPCA. His prize was a copy of *The Wind in the Willows*. For many years he worked for Collins, the publishers. It was during this period that his concern for conservation led him to write his first novel, *The Animals of Farthing Wood*, which won the Arts Council National Award for Children's Literature in 1980.

Colin has since published seven further books in his Farthing Wood/White Deer Park sequence: *In the Grip of Winter* (1981), *Fox's Feud* (1982), *The Fox Cub Bold* (1983), *The Siege of White Deer Park* (1985), *In the Path of the Storm* (1989), *Battle for the Park* (1992) and *Farthing Wood – The Adventure Begins* (1994). These stories were made into a highly successful animation series for the BBC. Other titles by him include *The Ram of Sweetriver* (1986), *The Beach Dogs* (1988), *Just Nuffin* (1989), *A Great Escape* (1990), *A Legacy of Ghosts* (1991) and the two previous books in the series featuring Sammy and Pinkie, *King of the Vagabonds* (1987) and *The City Cats* (1991).

Copycat

By the same author:

Colin Dann

COPYCAT

HUTCHINSON

London Sydney Auckland Johannesburg

First published in 1997

1 3 5 7 9 10 8 6 4 2

© Text Colin Dann 1997

Colin Dann has asserted his right under the Copyright, Designs and
Patents Act, 1988, to be identified as the author and illustrator of
this work

First published in the United Kingdom in 1997 by
Hutchinson Children's Books
Random House UK Limited
20 Vauxhall Bridge Road, London SW1V 2SA

Random House Australia (Pty) Limited
20 Alfred Street, Milsons Point, Sydney
New South Wales 2061, Australia

Random House New Zealand Limited
18 Poland Road, Glenfield
Auckland 10, New Zealand

Random House South Africa (Pty) Limited
Endulini, 5A Jubilee Road, Parktown 2193, South Africa

Random House UK Limited Reg. No. 954009

A CIP catalogue record for this book is available
from the British Library

Papers used by Random House UK Ltd are
natural, recyclable products made from wood grown
in sustainable forests.
The manufacturing processes conform to the environmental
regulations of the country of origin.

ISBN: 0 09 176509 9

Typeset in Baskerville by
Palimpsest Book Production Limited,
Polmont, Stirlingshire

Printed and bound in Great Britain by
Creative Print and Design, Ebbw Vale, Wales

Contents

For Colin and Liz

— 1 —

Kittens no more

'Well, Pinkie,' Sammy said to the little white cat, 'the cold weather's over. We should think about moving.'

Pinkie was washing her face, licking a paw and rubbing it across her pink nose and ears. Her blue eyes opened as she paused in her cleaning to look at her mate. 'What's the rush?' she asked lazily. 'We've been snug here, haven't we?'

The male tabby sat on his haunches. 'The youngsters are restless. They're wandering farther than they used to. They need to explore.'

'Oh yes – they get that from you,' Pinkie answered. She stood up and stretched in a patch of spring sunlight. The clump of thick bamboo where they had made their den rustled slightly in a warm breeze. 'The park's wide enough to satisfy their curiosity. Fern and Moss seem quite happy here.'

'For a while maybe,' Sammy said. 'But their brother has adventure on his mind. Little Sammy won't be checked for long.'

Pinkie gave Sammy her full attention. He was not a handsome cat. The uneven markings on his face marred his looks: in particular one broad stripe that ran from one corner to another seemed as if it had been added as an afterthought, crossing out what was already there. But Pinkie loved that face and she purred.

'All right, Sammy,' she said agreeably.

The pair of cats had been living in London's Regent's Park since before the winter. It was a safe haven for them in the great city and their kittens had been born and nurtured there. But Sammy had a roving nature and wanted a change, sure he could make his little family and himself comfortable elsewhere. He began to scout around.

A few days later, a change came about that neither Sammy nor Pinkie could have foreseen. The local council – as well as many neighbouring ones – had long been aware of the problem of strays, which were believed to pose a health hazard. A spiralling increase in numbers, especially of cats, had led to a decision to take drastic action. As many as possible were to be rounded up, and then either neutered or destroyed. Some people thought it a harsh solution, but even they had to admit that things could no longer remain as they were. So teams of control officers equipped with vans, snares, crates and other essentials were dispersed throughout the city. The London parks were targeted as some of the chief areas of concern.

One April afternoon Sammy, Pinkie and the youngsters were dozing near their den – not in a group, but scattered around within sight of each other. They had all eaten and they were feeling drowsy and lazy. Sammy was the first to hear the thud of heavy footsteps. A number of men, dressed alike in navy blue overalls, were stamping quickly towards them. Sammy recognized the threat at once and called a warning.

'Pinkie! Kittens! Run! Run!'

Pinkie didn't need to be told twice. She was on her

feet and racing after Sammy all in one swift movement. Together they ran like the wind. They were nearly at the other side of the park before Pinkie turned round to check on the youngsters.

'The kittens – they're not behind us,' Pinkie wailed. 'Sammy, you must go back for them.'

Sammy knew at once what he had to do. 'Pinkie, hide behind that hedge and stay very still,' he warned his mate. 'You'll be safe there for a while. I'll come back as soon as I've found them.'

He moved cautiously, back across the park, darting from behind one tree, bush or hedge to the next, never venturing out in the open, until finally he reached the site near the den. All was quiet. The men seemed to have disappeared, but Sammy did not let down his guard. He hunted for the kittens in all the most likely places, and then in the unlikely ones, but there was no sign of Little Sammy, Fern or Moss. It was beginning to get dark, and Sammy knew he must return to Pinkie.

She was still hiding in the hedge where he had left her, looking worried as if anticipating the news.

'They're nowhere to be seen,' said Sammy sadly. 'We can only hope that they've escaped in another direction.'

Pinkie was greatly distressed. 'But – but what if they've been captured?'

'If that's true, there's nothing we can do,' Sammy confessed. 'But we must get used to being alone again. The kittens have gone. And we're still in danger.'

Pinkie looked at him sadly. 'You mean –?'

Sammy licked Pinkie's fur, trying to calm her, and said, 'I'm sure those humans will come back, and we have to make sure we're not anywhere around when they do. We must save ourselves. It will be just you and me, Pinkie, the way it used to be. And we can have more kittens when we know we're safe,' Sammy added. 'We have no choice now but to go on our travels once again.'

— 2 —

Buster

Pinkie still yearned for her lost family. She couldn't accept that the youngsters had gone from her life for good. Supposing somehow they managed to return and found that she and their father had moved away? What would become of them?

'Sammy, we can't just go wandering,' she pleaded. 'Where would we go? We don't know anywhere else.'

'Oh, Pinkie, how can you say that? Have you forgotten the great journey I once made to find you? Is it so long ago? I roamed all over the city and understand its ways. Depend on me. You won't come to any harm.'

'Of course I hadn't forgotten that,' she answered. 'But you were on the move all the time. You didn't make a home anywhere.'

'I saw plenty of places where I could have,' Sammy told her. 'Look, I know how you're thinking. You can't get Fern, Moss and Little Sammy out of your mind. Neither can I. But, Pinkie, they won't be coming back. I don't know who those men were or what their purpose was. But they wanted to catch as many cats as they could. They would have had us too if I hadn't been so alert. There was a menace about them and you can be sure they didn't have our interests at heart.'

'Yes,' Pinkie whispered. 'I know. You're right. It was just . . . just a mother cat's feelings.'

Later that day Sammy caught a pigeon. Pinkie was uninterested. 'You must eat,' Sammy urged her. 'We shall need all our strength. I want to set off at dusk, and we don't know where our next meal will come from.'

Pinkie ate obediently but without relish. Sammy paced up and down alongside the high hedge. As the light began to fade he led Pinkie across the park, avoiding the wide open spaces. They reached another quarter. On the edge of the park there was a road with houses and parked cars.

'So far so good,' Sammy murmured. The words were hardly out of his mouth when a tremendous commotion broke out behind them.

'What is it?' Pinkie shrilled. Birds rocketed from the treetops, squirrels shinned up the trunks. Startled cries of birds and animals spread all around them as the tramp of heavy boots sounded once more, echoing horribly as they approached. Suddenly a feline scream made the cats' blood run cold. Sammy knew it was the last desperate cry of a cornered animal.

'They're back!' he cried. He was dreadfully frightened and began to run blindly towards the road. Pinkie followed him instinctively, but Sammy wasn't thinking properly in his panic and almost blundered into the path of another group of men emerging from a van.

'Catch it!' one of the men bellowed and another made a lunge at the terrified Sammy, who darted just out of reach and raced on along the pavement.

Pinkie dived under a parked car and cowered in its shadow, unable to see where best to run.

'This way!' a cat voice hissed at her from the other side of the road. She glanced up and saw a tabby, smaller and fluffier than Sammy, poised on the kerb. She hesitated only for a second. Where was Sammy? Then the boots came crunching in her direction again and she pelted across the road without even thinking about the traffic. The strange tabby scampered ahead, past houses and gardens, Pinkie close behind. Then Sammy came running towards them.

'Sammy!' Pinkie called anxiously.

The smaller tabby half turned. 'Your mate?' he asked. 'Yes.'

'OK. In here.' He jumped over a low wall into one of the gardens, ran towards the house and disappeared inside through a hole in a side door. Pinkie and Sammy were close behind and followed him. They didn't know where they were, but the house was silent, dark and comforting.

'I'm Buster,' came the tabby's voice. 'It's Sammy and –?'

'Pinkie.'

'Right. Pinkie. Well, this is where I live, Sammy and Pinkie. We're on our own. My master's not home, so you can relax.'

The din in the park was scarcely noticeable in the house and the two fugitives were able to calm down.

'You very nearly came croppers, the two of you,' Buster commented after a moment.

Sammy saw they were in a kitchen. He remembered very well how a kitchen looked. 'You've really done us a good turn,' he said gratefully to the stranger. 'Pinkie and I were planning to move away, but we weren't quick enough. Our kittens were taken earlier. Have you seen those men before?'

'Frequently. Don't you know about them?'

'Nothing. How could we?'

Buster showed surprise. 'Well, they've been around

often enough recently. They're collecting strays. Surely you've heard about the purge? All the cats – and dogs – along here know about it. Where have you come from, then?'

Sammy explained.

'Hm. Maybe you've been lucky,' Buster remarked. 'Now, make yourselves comfortable. You can lie down here on the mat by the table. You might as well. You'll be here for a while.'

'Where do they take the – the strays?' Pinkie asked. 'What do they do with them?'

'Who knows?' Buster grunted.

The cats, by now accustomed to the poor light, began to examine each other more closely. Buster was spotlessly clean and well groomed.

'You've the perfect bolt-hole here for avoiding capture,' Sammy said.

'I have,' the tabby agreed. 'But they wouldn't come after me anyway. I'm not a stray. There are still plenty of animals like you to keep those humans busy. Your numbers seem to grow all the time. I suppose that's the reason for this purge. Then along come the vans and those men dressed all the same. Tramp! Tramp!' he said, imitating the sound of the stomping boots.

'Don't,' Pinkie begged. 'It's too horrid.'

Sammy was puzzled. 'How do the men know which cats are strays and which are like you – I mean . . .'

'Pets?'

'Yes.' Sammy knew the word. 'Pets.'

Buster was amused. 'Well, look at you,' he chuckled. 'Isn't it obvious? You're like wild animals compared with me.'

There might have been something of an insult in the tabby's words but Sammy quickly realized their truth. He knew enough of human intelligence to accept that this distinction would be sufficient for clever humankind. He was deeply impressed by the idea and actually began to see Pinkie through different eyes as he looked from her to Buster and back again.

Pinkie reacted differently. 'You're a cosseted cat,' she retorted. 'Sammy and I have to do the best we can for ourselves without any other creature's help. And I wouldn't have it another way even if I could.' She wasn't used to sitting in human dwellings and the unusual warmth and cleanliness made her uneasy. 'When will your master return?' she asked nervously.

'Not till it's dark,' Buster replied. 'Don't worry, you're safe for the moment.' He got into his basket and appeared to be ready for sleep.

'But we can't stay here!' Pinkie mewed. 'You saved our skins, Buster, and we shan't forget it. We're out of place, though. We have to leave. We shall be discovered.' She was very jittery.

'Relax,' Buster soothed her. 'There's nothing to be afraid of here. I'll see to it. I'll know when my master's coming and I'll hide you.'

'We don't want to be hidden! Do we, Sammy?' Pinkie begged her mate. 'We want to go.'

'Wait. Wait, Pinkie,' Sammy said coolly. 'We can't go anywhere until we know the risk of capture has passed.'

'Exactly,' purred Buster. 'I'll look after you. You can share my food. See that tall cupboard? There's a big space behind it where you can hide while my meal is being prepared. I used to hunt for mice round there. Never found any, though. It's the perfect place for you two. Afterwards, when I'm left to myself – out you come again! And then we'll make plans. I'll try to think of a way to help.' He began to lick his chest fur in a methodical way. He was quite in control of the situation.

*   *   *

Shortly after dark the room was swept momentarily by a brilliant light. Pinkie scurried to the hiding place at once. Buster got up, stretched and yawned. 'The master's back,' he said. He knew the light meant the man's car had turned into the drive.

'Will he come in here first?' Sammy hissed.

'No, not straight away. You've plenty of time.'

The front door banged. Buster's owner's footsteps sounded in the hall, then the cats heard the creak of the stairs. The footsteps continued overhead. There was the noise of running water. 'He'll come soon now,' Buster announced. Sammy crept behind the cupboard and huddled beside Pinkie.

A young man opened the kitchen door, flicked on the light switch and began to talk to his pet. 'There you are, then.' Buster threaded his way in and out of the man's legs, his tail held high. 'I suppose you're hungry, like me? Yes, that's it. We'll get it all ready. Now, don't trip me up, good boy.'

To Sammy and Pinkie, hidden but wary and tense, the man's presence in the kitchen seemed to last an eternity. Two or three times Pinkie almost fled from cover when the man approached the cupboard. Somehow she managed to keep a grip on herself and at last the man took his own meal on a tray out of the room, switching off the light.

Buster called them. 'There's food here. I left you some. I usually go with him now. I'll be brought back here later when he goes to bed. After you've eaten, you'd better keep out of sight.' He trotted away to his human companion.

Sammy and Pinkie appreciated what little Buster hadn't eaten of the cat food. Then Pinkie said, 'I don't like it here. Let's go *now* – the way we came in.'

But Sammy said, 'I'm tired. And it's warm in here.

We can't come to any harm. Don't you want to see if Buster comes up with an idea?'

'Oh – Buster!' she scoffed. 'What does he know about what we want? You heard what he thinks of us. He's so superior.'

'No. No, I don't think so,' Sammy disagreed. 'We're different, that's all. You and I have to get right away from this area, from the city itself if we can. Otherwise we'll always be under threat. Buster does understand that. I'm willing to wait and hear what he has to say about it. He might be able to help. How about it?'

Pinkie sighed. 'Why ask? I know when your mind's made up.'

— 3 —

On the move again

Buster's return to the kitchen was hours away. In the meantime Sammy and Pinkie tried to doze. Eventually the pet tabby's owner felt ready for bed and Buster was carried to his basket and given a good-night cuddle. The kitchen door was closed soon after and the man retired upstairs.

'Come on. Now's the time,' Buster called.

Sammy and Pinkie emerged eagerly.

'I've thought of the perfect way to get you out of your difficulties,' Buster announced. 'I'll arrange for my master to take you.'

'What?' Pinkie screeched. 'What are you talking about?'

'Patience,' Buster soothed her. 'Let me explain.'

'It'll need some explaining,' the white cat retorted. 'We don't want any involvement with humans.'

Buster gave her a long-suffering look and even Sammy was irritated. 'Pinkie, *please.*'

'If you'll just listen,' Buster sighed. 'My master is the key to it all. He has a car.' He wiped a paw across his whiskers. 'Those machines travel at quite unimaginable speed. It could take you anywhere.' He paused and looked at the cats dramatically.

'Out of the city altogether?' Sammy asked.

'Very probably. When my master comes back in the evening there are often strange scents all over the car, not at all like those from the city. So it's a good guess it has travelled a long way.'

'Why ever would your master want *us* in his car?' Pinkie demanded. 'He doesn't even know about us.'

'Of course he doesn't,' Buster answered. 'And he won't.'

'But how would we get inside without him knowing?' Sammy asked, mystified.

'Simple. There are plenty of plants in the garden you can hide amongst. Then, as my master prepares to leave, I distract him. I know how to do *that.* Works every time. You two run up and jump in. There are rugs and all sorts of things you can burrow under in the back.'

'No,' said Pinkie. 'We won't be doing that. We'd be trapping ourselves. How would we get out again? Sammy and I have had one ordeal of that sort already and one that I shall never forget. I want nothing to do with humans or their machines. I'd rather we got away from here at our own pace.'

'Don't be so hasty,' Sammy cautioned. 'I have more experience of humans than you have. There's nothing to fear from one of the kind who keeps a cat for a pet! I think Buster's plan is a good one. The best we can hope for, anyway. It'd save us a lot of hardship and difficulty and worry – imagine what it would be like creeping along bit by bit and trying to dodge those patrols every day.'

'I'm only trying to help,' Buster assured Pinkie. 'But if you prefer to –'

'It's all right,' Sammy told him decisively. 'Pinkie will see sense. She's a very clever cat. And, of course, naturally wary.'

'Very understandable,' said Buster.

Pinkie was mollified. She saw there was no more to be said. 'Well, we'd better go back to our new den for now,' she sighed. 'We don't want to be found lying here in the morning.'

But of course there was no question of that. Long before the young man rose, Buster had taken Sammy and Pinkie through the cat-flap to the garden and shown them the best place to lie in wait near the car.

'You'll be quite unobserved there,' he told them as they screened themselves behind the foliage of a thick shrub. 'I hope you won't have to wait too long. I'm sorry there's nothing to eat.'

'You've done more than enough,' Sammy assured him. 'How many other animals have you helped?'

'Others? None, actually.'

'Then why us?' asked Pinkie.

'I just happened to be on the spot at the right time,' Buster explained. 'I saw your predicament. Who wouldn't come to the aid of a brother creature if he could? Besides, it's interesting to see the other side of life.'

'Oh. You mean us semi-wild beasts?' Sammy joked.

'I wouldn't put it quite like that. You have your lifestyle, I have mine. Doesn't mean we all have to ignore each other, does it?' His friendship was perfectly genuine and he added, 'I'm only sorry we're separating so soon after we met. Good luck.' With a farewell miaow, Buster went back indoors.

Sammy was aglow. 'What a delightful animal,' he purred. 'Human care and consideration have made him like that. He doesn't have any battles to fight. Life's no struggle for him. We must strike him as coarse and hard by comparison.'

Pinkie was offended. 'Speak for yourself,' she said

indignantly. 'But you've certainly fallen under his spell, haven't you? Perhaps you envy him?'

'No. Not envy,' Sammy answered. 'I was a pet once and I turned my back on that way of life. To be free and independent is everything to me. You know that already. But I sometimes feel I'd like to be – well, just a little more respectable.'

The cats lapsed into silence, thinking their own thoughts. Pinkie wasn't entirely happy about this interlude with a domestic pet. She could see that it had had an unexpected influence on Sammy which perhaps didn't bode well for the future. She was impatient to be away before any more harm might be done.

The cats listened to the various noises from inside the house and from the street. Even now, in this private garden, they feared the return of the tramp! tramp! of those heavy boots. So it was a relief of sorts when the young man appeared, carrying his case ready for work. He opened one of the car's rear doors and put his case on the floor, and at that moment Buster began to miaow urgently from the low garden wall. The man turned, his hand still on the door. Buster called some more.

'What is it? What do you want?' the man laughed. 'Have you found something there?' He strolled over and tickled his pet behind the ear. Sammy and Pinkie shot from cover and leapt inside the car. They clawed frantically at the rugs, desperate to get out of sight. Fortunately the car's back seat, which was rarely used, was strewn with an accumulation of paper, packages and a few items of clothing as well as the two thick car rugs. So the cats, hearts a-flutter, were easily able to make themselves invisible.

Buster watched carefully until they were safe and then instantly appeared to lose all interest in his master.

He jumped off the wall and went trotting along the pavement to next door's garden. The young man, who was quite used to his pet's ways, stepped up to his car, shut the door on Sammy and Pinkie and got into the driving seat. The cats' journey was about to begin.

They remained absolutely still and quiet. The car stopped several times, sometimes briefly, sometimes for lengthy periods. The young man was a sales representative and had many calls to make on his customers. But, for as long as the din of the city could be heard each time the car stopped, Sammy prevented Pinkie from moving. He wanted to be sure they had quit the city before stirring, because that was the only way he would be satisfied that he and Pinkie were beyond the reach of the vans, the snares and the tramping boots. So they waited for the quieter, more peaceful sounds they recalled from their earlier life in the countryside.

They tried to catnap, but the jolting of the car, their nagging stomachs and their anxiety made it impossible. But they were not alone in feeling the demands of hunger. Around midday the salesman pulled into a pub car park for a hasty lunch.

The pub overlooked a river and the surroundings were peaceful. The man got out, locked the car and strode away. The general quietness was soon noticeable to the two cats.

'I think this is it,' Sammy said excitedly. 'I think we've made it, Pinkie. We've left the city behind!'

Cautiously they sat up and looked out of the nearest window. There were no people visible, no moving vehicles and no massed buildings crowding the roadside. The river's murmur was just audible.

'The man's going to get a big surprise when he comes back,' Pinkie said. 'I hope nothing goes wrong now.'

'Don't worry,' Sammy said. 'We haven't come all this way to let things slip at the last moment. We won't have much time. We must jump just as soon as the door begins to open.'

There was a final tense wait. Luckily the young salesman had a busy day and couldn't spare long for his break. A sandwich and a fruit juice was all he had time for. He came striding across the car park. The cats were ready. The driver's door opened and Sammy and Pinkie fled, almost leaping on top of the man in their haste to get through the gap. Buster's owner staggered and cried out.

'Good God! What on earth . . . ?' He spun round, still in a state of shock, in an effort to see what had struck him, and spotted the cats scampering across the car park towards the river. His jaw dropped and he watched them in a complete daze. It was a long time before he was able to collect his thoughts.

Sammy led the way to the river bank. The first priority was to get under cover again. He and Pinkie had no way of knowing whether the man would give chase. There were some strollers on the towpath by the river. The cats avoided them and ran in amongst some rank weeds. A train abruptly thundered across a nearby bridge. On the other side of the river there was a cluster of tall buildings along the waterfront. New ones were under construction, and the noise of machinery and human shouts leapt the width of water and assailed the cats' ears.

'I don't think we've escaped the city,' Pinkie wailed. 'Look, Sammy, we're still in its clutches!'

—4—

'We have to change'

Sammy tried to be cheerful. 'We don't have to worry,' he said. 'We've got all this water between us and that . . . that . . .'

'Menace?' Pinkie suggested.

'Yes, well we must simply stay on this side,' he countered. 'Maybe it's different over here.'

'We've hardly begun to look yet.'

'No. There's plenty of time for exploring. We're not under any threat right now. And if you feel anything like me, the main thought in your mind at this moment is food.'

Pinkie had no argument with that. Both cats were skilful hunters and they soon found there were voles and mice to be had in the long grass by the river. With hunger partly satisfied, Sammy began to think about finding a temporary den. Always in his thoughts was the need for a safe haven. He didn't dare give voice to his fear that he and Pinkie might even now be within reach of the men who were rounding up the strays. He had longed to have the countryside around him again, but it was all too obvious that he hadn't achieved his desire.

'We mustn't make our next den on the ground,' he blurted out without considering.

'So you *do* think we're still at risk,' Pinkie accused him. 'Oh, what are we going to do now?'

'We're going to climb, that's what we're going to do,' Sammy answered, mustering all his self-confidence. 'We've got to go high. There's safety in height.'

'I agree with you. But could we sleep in a tree?'

'Might not have to be a tree,' Sammy pointed out. 'It could be anything. A roof of a – a – shed or something.'

'There'd be no shelter on a roof.'

'Perhaps not. We must look around.'

The cats kept to the long grass and weeds until the towpath was free of people. Then they used the path themselves, from where it was much easier to examine their surroundings. A long wall on their left separated the back gardens of a row of houses from the riverside, and at the end of the row there was a church.

'We could start by getting on top of that wall,' Pinkie suggested. 'We could see a lot from there.' She sighed. 'If we could only jump that high.'

'There's a way up over there – look.' Sammy hastened forward to where a clump of sallow with thin wavy branches grew close against the wall. He thought it just might bear their weight. 'I'll go first,' he said. 'I'm heavier than you, so if I can make it . . .'

With a bound he was up amongst the budding branches with their fluffy catkins. The willowy stems shook dangerously but, balancing himself with his tail, Sammy scrambled clear and climbed to the top of the wall. Pinkie followed immediately and the cats sat side by side surveying the scene in front of them.

'Human dwellings,' the little white cat summed up. 'We can't hope for anything there.'

'Don't be so sure,' Sammy answered. 'There could be

all sorts of snug, secret little places in those gardens that would suit us very well.'

Pinkie, as usual, wasn't keen to be anywhere near humans. 'I don't want to be within reach of their eager prying eyes,' she said.

'Oh, Pinkie!' the tabby exclaimed. 'Don't be so awkward. There are many humans who are kindly towards animals. *All* animals,' he added. 'Trust me. You don't have to see every one as your enemy.'

'I don't,' she answered. 'I just prefer to keep them at a distance.'

'But they could be useful to us,' Sammy reminded her. 'How did we get here, after all? And, don't you remember, when we first discovered each other, how you used to accept food from one of the kindly ones?'

'Yes, yes. I know. We can use them in some ways. But only on our terms. I don't want to be adopted.'

Sammy said no more just then. But in fact he had some very different ideas in his mind. The impression made on him by Buster was still vivid. Sammy had begun to develop his own theory about the benefits of behaving like a human's pet.

In one garden he saw a shed completely covered by a climbing plant which had wrapped its mass of stems all over the sides and roof like a lot of green tentacles. 'That seems like an ideal shelter for the two of us for now,' he murmured. 'We'd keep warm in there tonight. What d'you think, Pinkie?'

'There doesn't seem to be anything better,' she replied without enthusiasm. 'But we needn't go there till dark, need we? We don't want to be spotted.'

Sammy was amused. There they were, the two of them, perched on top of a high wall overlooking every house in the row. How much more visible could

they get? 'All right, Pinkie,' he chuckled. 'Whatever
you say.'

For the rest of the daylight hours the cats returned to
the riverside and kept out of sight in the long grass. The
anxiety in the car during their long journey earlier in the
day had tired them and they were both eager to rest. At
dusk Sammy led the way along the wall to the chosen
retreat. They jumped down into the garden and stepped
carefully across to the shed. It was easy to climb to the
roof and then, under the matted strands of the plant,
to find a space that was hidden, dry and comfortable.
A cushion of dead leaves, trapped by the thick tendrils,
made a safe place to lie on.

During the night the call of an owl and the snuffling
of a roving hedgehog were the only sounds that reached
their ears. True to their nature, the cats dozed and woke
and dozed again. But towards daybreak they were rudely
awakened. It began to rain heavily. Although they were
fairly well protected from the worst of the weather,
the drumming of the raindrops on the wooden roof
couldn't be ignored. Pinkie stirred.

'Why move?' Sammy checked her. 'We'll stay drier in
here than almost anywhere else.'

'It'll be daylight soon. We *have* to move,' was her
answer.

'Whatever for? No one knows we're here, so no one
will come searching for us.'

Pinkie simply wasn't happy to remain in the vicinity of
humans. She was restless and peered through the screen
of greenery, looking nervously in each direction.

'At least wait while this rain is so heavy,' Sammy per-
suaded her. 'You'd get soaked out there in no time.'

Pinkie certainly didn't relish that prospect and tried
to be still. Daylight came and the rain didn't ease up.

It began to penetrate the climbing plant's protection. The cats felt cold and miserable.

'There's no advantage in this,' Pinkie declared and started to pull herself free of the drenched vegetation. All at once she stopped. Though fully exposed to the lashing rain, suddenly she seemed unaware of it. She was listening to a tramp! tramp! of steps down the road.

'It can't be!' Sammy hissed and tried to crawl even further into the jungle of stems.

Pinkie was frozen to the spot. She couldn't decide whether to run or clamber back in with Sammy. 'Pinkie! Pinkie! Hide yourself!' Sammy begged. 'Stay with me!' She dived in by his side, trembling violently, unable to speak. Now new frightening noises were added to the beating raindrops and the tramping feet. The bell of the church at the end of the road began to toll and a band of bugles and drums struck up in time to the marching footsteps. The frantic pair of cats wondered what new terror was being unleashed against them and their kind. Unhappily they couldn't know they were hearing the sounds of a scout troop's Sunday church parade.

The noise blared and thumped for a while, then abruptly ceased. Only the church bell continued to chime, while the cruel rain slackened to a patter. It was an age before the cats even felt safe enough to talk.

'We're still . . . in the . . . city,' Pinkie gasped. 'We'll never . . . get away.' She shuddered.

'We escaped the men last time,' Sammy said. 'We can do so again.'

'And again and again?' Pinkie said. 'How many times before they catch us in the end?'

Sammy got up and shook himself. He looked at his mate. Her fur was saturated by the rain and stuck all over with rotting leaves and twigs. He could hardly glimpse a suggestion of white on her coat. She was filthy and he realized he must look much the same. 'We have to change our habits,' he said emphatically. 'There's only one way we can avoid capture indefinitely and that's by fooling the patrols into thinking we're pets.' He had been coming to this conclusion in his own mind for a long while. Now he had finally accepted it, he felt much more optimistic.

'How can we possibly . . . ?' Pinkie began.

'Because we must,' he answered. 'We're too vulnerable as we are. Look at me. How could I be mistaken for anything but a stray? We're both dirty, unkempt and undernourished. We haven't escaped from the city entirely, as we hoped. We've simply been brought to another, rather quieter part of it. So we have to revise our plans.'

Pinkie listened attentively. Sammy could be so clever. The rain stopped altogether and the sun broke through the massed clouds. A patch of sunlight in the garden attracted them. They needed to dry off.

'Come on,' Sammy said. 'I'll explain when we get there. We can lie against the fence. We shouldn't be disturbed.'

They jumped from the shed roof. The morning was warming up. They made sure no people or other animals were nearby. Then they ran to the sunny patch and lay down gratefully where the sun's rays could bathe them.

'Now,' Sammy began importantly, 'the first thing we have to do is to improve our appearance. We must always look clean and beautifully groomed. We must be really meticulous about it. We want to look appealing to the human eye. Like Buster. We haven't taken proper care of ourselves before. I *was* a pet once so I have some idea how to go about it. You never were so I shall have to teach you. We've been living rough and, as you've known nothing else, you've always been wild. I've become that way myself, but it's going to be more

difficult for you to change. And, Pinkie, you must, you
know. Otherwise there's a risk I'd be overlooked while
you were taken.'

Pinkie began to tremble again as Sammy's words sank
in. The prospect of such a separation was disturbing. 'I
do clean myself,' she protested. 'But – but . . .'

'But you couldn't pass for a pet,' Sammy finished for
her. 'So we have a lot to do. We have to look like pets
and we have to behave like them too. First we must have
a base. A proper one. No more sleeping in the open or
amongst plants.'

'You mean somewhere like the hut in Quartermile
Field?' Pinkie queried. She was referring to her old
home in the country where she had first encountered
Sammy.

'Maybe, but a little grander, I think. Would a pet live
in a broken-down, abandoned place like that? No. You
see,' said Sammy, 'in order to look like a pet you have
to live like one.'

Pinkie bridled at this. 'Preposterous! I've never lived
like a pet and wouldn't know how to. And I'm too old
to start now!'

'It's the only way, Pinkie, believe me,' Sammy urged
her. 'I'll help you all I can. I promise you we'll remain
quite independent. But we must be more particular. I'll
work it all out somehow. You just leave it to me.'

Pinkie was silent. She didn't believe Sammy's plan
could be carried out. But there was no denying that her
clever tabby mate had performed some extraordinary
feats in the past. All she could do now was to wait and
see if he was capable of adding to them.

— 5 —

You scratch my back

Sammy felt his fur warm and dry in the sunshine. He got up and shook himself energetically. Fragments of leaf and stalk showered to the ground. 'Ugh! I can smell I'm dirty,' he muttered, squatting again. Using his paws and especially his tongue he gave himself a thorough clean-up. 'That's better,' he said. 'How do I look?'

Pinkie had been watching his elaborate toilet with interest. 'Like a show cat,' she joked.

'Hardly.' He gave her a cat smile, closing his eyes. 'Still, we can start as we mean to go on.' He moved close to Pinkie and began to lick her face. Pinkie purred and nuzzled him. But when Sammy transferred his tongue to her back fur she jumped up.

'You don't need to groom me!' she hissed. 'I know how to keep clean.'

'Just trying to help,' he murmured and watched her as she went through her programme. 'Your coat's not as white as it used to be,' he remarked afterwards.

'That's age. I'm not a youngster any more,' Pinkie reminded him. 'And don't be so critical.'

'But we have to be,' he responded. 'It's only when we can look at each other with admiration that we'll know we're safe.'

Pinkie was hurt. 'I hope you're not going to take

this plan of yours too far,' she said. 'I can only be what I am.'

'Of course. It's all right. There's plenty of time to learn. I said I'd teach you.'

Pinkie wasn't reassured. 'I can't learn to grow whiter fur,' she objected. But Sammy wasn't listening. He was looking away, his thoughts on something else.

'I must explore,' he was saying to himself. 'We need proper food and shelter.' He turned and looked at his companion. 'We can make use of the humans. Just as you said, Pinkie. I expect it'll be better if I go alone to begin with? I'll have to go really close to the houses to find what we need, and I know how you feel about that. Will you stay around here?'

'That depends,' Pinkie answered. 'It may not remain quiet.'

'No. Well, you'll know what to do if it doesn't. I'll leave you now. We won't lose each other. You know my call.'

Pinkie watched Sammy climb the fence and drop into the neighbouring garden. In his absence she moved. She believed she was vulnerable and preferred to be nearer the long wall so as to be able to reach her escape route if necessary.

Sammy was thinking of Buster and his wonderful little private door. What a perfect arrangement for any cat: to have the freedom to come and go as you pleased, yet have all the benefits of good food, warmth and comfort provided for you into the bargain. Why was Buster so special? Or were there other pets as fortunate? And if so . . . were there any around here? He approached the nearest house with the utmost caution. In the daylight boldness had to be used sparingly.

'Nothing of interest here,' he said to himself. 'I'll go into the next garden.' There was only a low wall to negotiate this time. Sammy thought he detected the scent of a dog and made a hasty scan of the outside of the house, then progressed to the neighbouring garden. 'This is like my kitten days,' he chuckled, 'when I first started to discover the world beyond my birthplace. Ah now – here's something. There's definitely another cat around and it's a male. His smell's everywhere.' He looked all over the garden. The cat was absent but the plants, a small tree and a patio at the back of the house all bore the strongest marks that it was another animal's territory.

'He must be roaming elsewhere,' Sammy told himself, 'otherwise he'd certainly suspect my presence.' There was no cat-flap at the back of the house and Sammy didn't have the confidence to go round to the front. That would bring him close to the very road where the march had taken place earlier. Any exploring on that side would have to wait until nightfall.

The next garden he went into had evidence of at least two cats and possibly more. One scent predominated. Fainter taints of other animsls became more marked as Sammy inched towards the house. There was not a sound from inside the building, human or otherwise.

'A door! A private cat door!' Sammy suddenly cried in excitement as he spied a cat-flap, almost exactly like Buster's. It was set at ground level into a large glass door that ran the width of one room, in front of which was a paved area with garden furniture. Sammy felt sufficiently sure that the house was at present empty to go right up to the glass door and peer through. The slightest hint of a sound or movement inside would have sent him flying, but all was still and quiet. The room he looked into was a sitting-room. It seemed comfortable and inviting, with soft chairs and rugs begging to be curled up on and, just inside the glass door, an animal's

food-bowl containing some crumbs left over from a
recent meal.

'Pinkie and I could do with some of that kind of stuff,'
Sammy muttered. 'Dare I go in and polish it off?' There
didn't appear to be any danger. He looked all round
once more, then pushed the flap with his head. It
opened easily and, a second later, Sammy was licking the
food-bowl clean. Once inside the house, it didn't need
a lot more courage for Sammy to want to nose around.
Maybe there was some more food somewhere?

He stepped to the doorway. Food smells of another
kind wafted to him from the kitchen so that was where
he headed next. There was a water-bowl in there but no
more food to be seen. Sammy took a drink. There was
no doubting this was the house of the cat whose scent
was so strong in the garden, for his smell was everywhere
in the house too. Sammy knew the animal could return
at any time but he wasn't afraid of any mere cat. So, since
the cat's owner wasn't at home, he decided to continue
to explore. There was one more room on the ground
floor which also smelt of food. It was the dining-room.
Sammy sat under the table, sniffing the tantalizing
aroma. Suddenly he heard a rattle. He ran instantly
back to the first room. A sleek black cat stood by the
patio door, having just slipped inside. Its hackles rose
at the sight of Sammy and it stared at him, motionless,
taking his measure. Sammy stood his ground. The black
cat was smaller than he was and he could tell it was on
its guard and more likely to flee than to fight.

'You live here?' Sammy asked mildly.

'Always.' A strange answer!

'You mean you were born here?'

'Of course I wasn't born here. I came from a pet shop
like the other cats.'

'Are there others living here too, then?' Sammy asked.

'Not at the moment. They've gone away. They often do. But *I* still live here and I get fed too.'

'Yes. I noticed. Why is it you don't go with the other cats, then?'

'Which other cats?'

'The ones who have gone away.'

'I don't know what you're talking about,' the black cat said. He had begun to relax. 'How would I know what the other cats do?'

Sammy came closer. There was no threat offered on either side. 'You said the others had gone away?' he quoted.

The black cat sat down. 'My owners. My owners have gone away,' he explained. 'That doesn't mean any cat has the right –'

'I'm not any cat,' Sammy interrupted. 'I'm different. And *I* didn't come from a pet shop.'

'No. You look like a stray.'

The significance of the last word, with all that it entailed for Sammy and Pinkie, sent a shiver of remembrance along the tabby's spine. 'I live independently, yes. With my mate. We prefer it that way. But I detest that word "stray".'

'What other word is there?'

Sammy said, 'What's your name? And who feeds you now?'

'Monty. What's yours?'

'Sammy. Aren't you going to tell me how you get fed?'

'You'd like to know that, wouldn't you? Just like the rest. All they think about is food.'

'The "rest" being the other cats?'

'Who else? I can't always eat the whole plateful at once; she puts out such a lot at a time. And then, of course, there they are sniffing around, hoping for

an extra meal. *I* can't keep them out. But they've no
right to –'

'Other cats come in here?' Sammy interjected.

'Well, they would, wouldn't they? Even when I'm here
sometimes. Oh, they'll wait until the girl's gone, but –'

'But you don't scare them off?'

The black cat looked uncomfortable. 'No. Well, I'm
not as rough and tough as some of them. Like *you*, I
suppose. But this is *my* home. And why do they think
they've the right to –'

'Strays or pets, the other cats?' Sammy blurted out.
He'd had an idea.

'Oh, they're nearly all so-called "pets" round here,'
Monty answered derisively. 'They don't behave much
like it, though. They're as greedy as . . . well, you
know . . .'

'The ones like me?' Sammy finished.

'What I meant was, the ones who try to catch their
own food,' Monty replied diplomatically.

'I could perhaps be of help to you,' Sammy offered
craftily, 'if you would be prepared to make it worth
my while.'

Monty's eyes narrowed. 'You help? How?'

'I think I could keep the unwanted callers away.'

'Oh yes? And what am I expected to do in return?'
the black cat asked suspiciously.

'I don't ask much. A portion of your unwanted food, a
dry place to lie . . .' Sammy stretched his legs, front pair
first, then the hind ones. He lifted a paw and licked it,
then rubbed it over his face. His air of nonchalance was
calculated and persuasive. Monty felt he had nothing
to lose.

'Doesn't sound a lot,' he admitted. 'How would you
go about driving off the intruders?'

'I'm a King Cat,' Sammy answered simply, referring

to the position of supremacy he had held when younger amongst a group of rivals. 'And I'm the son of a King Cat too.'

Monty didn't know what a King Cat was. He was and always had been a human's pet. But the title certainly sounded impressive. 'Oh,' he whispered, rather in awe of the tabby. 'Well, in that case . . .'

'Good,' said Sammy. 'Now, first things first. When is the food brought?'

'Mornings and evenings.'

'Ah. So you've had your first meal today?'

'Yes. And you found it, didn't you?'

'Me?' Sammy cried. 'Oh no. When I came in here there wasn't enough food left for a mouse.'

'So another came before you,' Monty growled. 'You see what I mean? They're in and out all the time. I can't stand guard here, can I? Of course, the girl thinks *I* eat it all. So she keeps putting out –'

'Too much for one?' Sammy finished for him. He blinked and smiled a cat smile. 'Yes, we'll have to make sure that continues, won't we?'

Monty stared, unsure if this was a threat.

'Well, look at me,' Sammy continued. 'This is how you look if you live off birds and mice. I want to look like you. Glossy and plump and contented. It's dangerous to look anything less these days, isn't it?'

Monty said, 'You mentioned a mate. Where is she? Hiding upstairs?'

'No, no. I came alone. We're strangers to the area and I needed to find us a safe spot. So I left her waiting. But there's no point in keeping her in suspense any longer. I'll go and tell her the good news. And we'll be back in time for the next feed.'

Monty gaped as Sammy slipped through the cat-flap. The tabby had settled affairs to his own satisfaction, but the black cat felt as though events had somehow overtaken him. 'Well,' he gulped. 'I'm not quite sure what I've done. He seems to think he has the right to –' He broke off, then muttered, 'And his mate too!'

—6—

I'll scratch yours

Sammy was very pleased with himself. At his first attempt he had found a cosy base and the promise of some good food for himself and Pinkie. Pets like Monty were easy to deal with. Things were looking up.

Pinkie wasn't where he had left her, and Sammy soon discovered why. A man was in the garden by the shed where they had spent the night and he had an Alsatian with him. Sammy sprang from the fence-top back into the neighbouring garden. He guessed Pinkie must have gone over the wall to the riverside. He called her and heard her answer, and they were soon reunited.

'To think we spent all night in there under the nose of that huge dog,' Pinkie said at once. 'We'll never be able to sleep there again.'

'Oh, we were quite safe,' Sammy answered airily. 'Pet dogs like that are usually kept indoors.' He thought of Molly, the gentle old mongrel he had been brought up with. 'Besides, it wouldn't have known we were there.'

'But afterwards?' Pinkie mewed. 'We were sunning ourselves right there by the fence. We could have been torn to pieces!'

'Nonsense,' Sammy soothed. 'Dogs of that kind are softer than they look. Anyway, let's forget it. Our problems are over.'

'How can that be?'

Sammy explained proudly about his arrangement with the black cat. To his disappointment Pinkie's reaction was guarded.

'Have you been careful enough? I wouldn't trust anything where humans are concerned.'

'There *are* no humans. They're away.'

'What about the one who brings the food?'

'There's no cause for alarm. The food is left. The girl doesn't stay around. The black cat told me. And we wouldn't put in an appearance until the house was empty.'

'Just when all the other cats in the neighbourhood are gathering.'

'Oh, Pinkie! You don't know that. Other cats come. But probably not in a group. They're all rivals for the food, aren't they? So they'd be trying to sneak in secretly where they could, wouldn't they, to cheat the rest? Anyway, I'm going to stop all that. That's the deal.'

'I hope you'll be a match for them.'

'They're just pets like Monty,' Sammy replied confidently. 'And I'm a fighter.'

Pinkie purred. 'Of course you are,' she said. 'And a winner too. *I* should know. I didn't mean to doubt you. You'll be tough enough for them all. Oh, how the sparks will fly!' She sounded gleeful.

Sammy looked at her smugly. 'Isn't it a clever plan?' He nuzzled her. 'Our lives will be transformed. Some of that good nourishing pet food every day and a warm dry place to sleep! We won't be vagabonds any more. And we won't be taken!'

Pinkie let him enjoy his feeling of success. She looked forward, as he did, to some good food. She ached for a really satisfying meal. But she had no intention of using

a human dwelling to sleep in. That was going too far.
You could get trapped like that. She would say nothing
for the moment. Sammy would find out soon enough
and, when he did, he would see the error of his ways.

They were both impatient for the evening. Their hunger
was sharpened by the promise of what was to come.
Sammy was content to hold on, but Pinkie was so
ravenous she went hunting on her own. By the river
bank she found a dead fish floating amongst some
reeds. It was a large fish and a lucky find. Pinkie
hooked it out and smelt it carefully. It wasn't particularly fresh but the strong odour made her mouth
run with water. She took a couple of bites. The flesh
was soft, almost rotten. Pinkie swallowed it easily. There
was enough meat on the bones for Sammy too. After
satisfying her immediate craving she ran back to fetch
him.

The news of Pinkie's find tempted him sorely. It
wasn't the kind of food they would be eating in future,
but there was still a good part of the day to endure
before Monty's food-bowl could be investigated.

'I'll come and have a look,' Sammy told his little
white-coated mate.

'Don't do yourself any favours,' Pinkie muttered but
Sammy didn't hear and she led him off at a run.

Sammy's nose picked up the smell of the half-eaten
fish before his eyes located it. When he saw it he
was angry. It was the perfect representation of everything about their present life he was determined to
change.

'It's disgusting,' he growled. 'I shan't touch it!'

'Please yourself,' Pinkie replied. 'There was a time
when you would have thought it a banquet.'

'No,' he said. 'There are some things I never would

have eaten. And neither of us is going to accept food like that again.'

Pinkie had her own views on that matter but she kept silent.

'Don't you see? You've got to think differently,' Sammy went on. 'The sort of cats we're going to be wouldn't give that . . . that object a second look.'

'Is that so?'

'It is. Remember: think like a pet so that you can act like a pet. It's perfectly simple.'

'It may be to you,' she retorted. 'I've passed too many seasons making out whichever way I can to be able to change so suddenly. There's such a thing as instinct.'

'Of course. But follow me; just do as I do. You'll get the hang of it.'

'I'll never get the hang of passing up a good meal,' Pinkie told him honestly. Sammy ignored the remark.

As the day wore on the tabby became more and more agitated. He could think of nothing but getting into Monty's garden, watching for the food delivery and then effortlessly ousting any competitors. He prowled up and down against the high wall, on the river side. Pinkie watched him irritably from her couch of weeds. Finally she said, 'Why on earth don't you go? You look like a caged beast. Perhaps the food is already there.'

Sammy looked at her sharply. 'D'you think so? We mustn't miss out. But it's still daylight.'

'Does the food come under cover of darkness?'

'I don't know.'

'Well then . . .'

'All right. We'll go now and take up the best places.' He spurted away as though his life depended on it. Pinkie had difficulty keeping up.

'This way, this way,' Sammy hissed when they reached Monty's garden, creeping through the clumps of plants in the flower bed and keeping close enough to the fence to feel his fur brushing it. They neared the house. The black cat wasn't anywhere to be seen, neither was there any sign or sound of a human presence. But, just ahead, under a shrub, squatting motionless as a sphinx, was another cat, a stocky black-and-white. It was facing the big glass door, so totally absorbed in watching that it wasn't aware of the newcomers. Sammy realized that he and Pinkie had come just in time. They inched along.

Suddenly Monty appeared, running down the centre of the lawn directly to his little door. He disappeared inside the house. Immediately the black-and-white cat got up, but Sammy ran to him with a low growl and blocked his path. The other animal recoiled, taken totally by surprise. Pinkie purred excitedly, waiting for fur to fly.

Monty ate busily. Every so often he paused to look outside. He suspected that other animals were around but he didn't know where they were lurking. He heard a snarl, then the angry sounds of a brief scrap. The black-and-white cat raced across the grass with Sammy in pursuit. The tabby drove it straight to the fence where it scrambled for sanctuary, its tail flicking nervously. But Sammy wasn't happy with that. He growled threateningly, preparing to launch himself. The black-and-white cat didn't wait around. It was gone in a trice.

'My!' Monty said to himself. 'This *is* an animal to be reckoned with.' He backed away from the food-bowl as though he'd been eating something that didn't belong to him.

Sammy, with Pinkie dancing around him, came to

claim his due. 'You see?' he said to Monty. 'Nothing easier, when you're determined.' He looked at the food. 'Have you finished here?'

'Er – yes.'

'Go on, Pinkie. There's plenty. Take what you want,' Sammy offered.

Pinkie, having already eaten the fish, ate sparingly, leaving the lion's share for the tabby. Sammy gulped it down greedily, keeping an eye on the garden in case another competitor should appear. None did. Monty hovered, unsure what was required of him. He soon found out.

'Will the girl be back?' Sammy demanded.

'Not till tomorrow.'

'Good. Show us where we can sleep.'

Pinkie started to intervene, but Sammy checked her. 'Be quiet, Pinkie. We have to know where to go so that we won't be disturbed.'

Monty was at a loss for suggestions. What did these two strays expect? A basket? A chair? What exactly?

'Where do you sleep?' Sammy asked, trying to chivvy him up. 'In here?'

'No. My bed's in the kitchen. But you can't –'

'Can't sleep in there?' Sammy finished for him. 'We don't want to. This room is quite comfortable enough for us. The floor will suit us fine – in fact, by comparison with what we're used to, it's the finest luxury for Pinkie and me.'

'No. Not Pinkie,' said his mate.

Sammy turned to look at her. 'What? What do you mean?'

'I mean I'm not sleeping in here.'

'Oh. What do you propose then? Somewhere even softer?' Sammy asked jocularly.

'Not at all. I'll take my chances in the open as I always

have. You'll never get me to lie in one of these human
"dens" like a mouse in a trap.'

'A trap? There's no trap. You have an escape route
where you came in,' Sammy argued. 'What about our
plan? I had it all worked out.'

'*Your* plan,' Pinkie corrected him. 'I appreciate the
food.' She looked at Monty. 'Thank you, stranger. It'll
make a big difference. As for a bed, I'll find my own.
Somewhere secluded and as dry as I can make it. But
not enclosed within a place built for humans and ringed
round with their . . . their trappings.'

Sammy was aghast. He'd never heard Pinkie in this
mood before. 'Are you going to leave me, then?' he
gasped. 'Go off on your own?'

'Well, that's what it amounts to, doesn't it, if you're
so set on sleeping indoors?' Pinkie answered coolly.

'But where will you go?'

'Can't say at present. I'll find somewhere.'

Sammy became irritated. 'Oh well, if that's your attitude . . . I've done my best for you, and all you do is
turn your nose up.'

Monty looked from one cat to the other, wondering
where all this was going to lead. He felt like a bystander
in his own home. Sammy was annoyed and offended.
He turned his back on Pinkie and deliberately walked
away towards the far end of the room. He began to wash
himself. Pinkie was quite still for a moment. However,
her determination matched Sammy's and, with some
reluctance, she stepped to the cat-flap.

'Tell him I shan't go far,' she murmured to Monty.
'He'll be able to find me easily.' She pushed herself
through the little door and was gone without a backward
glance. She was confident Sammy would soon come
after her.

But Pinkie had miscalculated. Sammy was stubborn

and, when Monty repeated the message, he said, 'It doesn't matter how far she goes. I shan't be looking for her.' The two cats were set on separate paths and neither was going to give way.

— 7 —

The Pub Cat

The black-and-white cat Sammy had chased away knew all the other cats in the road as well as several others who lived further afield and sometimes crossed his path.

His name was Domino. He was bigger than most, including Monty, and his size had made him respected amongst the pets. He had regularly taken food from Monty's bowl because, although he was fed adequately by his owners, he was greedy. He had never encountered an animal like Sammy before and had been immediately cowed by his fierce appearance. He decided to warn his acquaintances about the big tabby who had suddenly appeared on the scene. Two of these had been on the point of approaching Monty's garden when the sounds of the fight between Sammy and Domino made them turn tail. When the black-and-white cat made his escape he ran into them. One was a grey Burmese called Ling and the other a ginger called Spike. Both were rather docile creatures with mild manners who would always avoid a confrontation. They feared Domino even though he never attacked them because they accepted his supremacy so easily, so he had to make it clear he was in a friendly mood in order to prevent their scattering.

'Wait! I've got some news for you,' he called reassuringly. 'It'll be in your interests to listen.'

Ling and Spike, who were friends, hesitated. Was it something to do with the fight?

'There's a new cat around,' Domino told them. 'A real bruiser. He's after the food at Monty's and he's hanging around his garden. I didn't get a look in. He gave me quite a fright. Attacked me for no reason. I'd advise you to keep away from there for a while.'

Ling, who had a fat puckered sort of face, said, 'We heard the row. What's this cat look like?'

'A lean, hard tabby with an ugly mug. He looks as if he's been around.'

'Where did he come from?' Spike asked.

Domino snorted. 'I didn't stay to ask. If I see any of the others I'm going to warn them too. You do the same. He really looks as though he could be an unpleasant customer.'

Meanwhile the subject of this conversation was trying to sleep and finding it very difficult. As the evening shadows spread across Monty's garden Sammy, warm and well fed, dozed and started. He imagined every other moment that Pinkie was creeping through the cat-flap to join him. Yet each time his eyes blinked open and he looked towards the glass door, there was no one there. Monty had retired to his basket, unsure how to cope with the stranger who had so suddenly changed his life.

'Perhaps I'll find him gone in the morning,' Monty said to himself. 'He'll want to look for his mate.' But even as he thought it, he knew Sammy would demand the next lot of meat. The way he had dealt with Domino meant he had kept his side of the bargain. And if Domino couldn't stand up to him, none of the other visitors to the garden would either. So Sammy had already proved he was as good as his word. The rivalry for his – Monty's – food-bowl had been ended in one fell swoop. And that was something gained, anyway. 'But I hope the girl doesn't find him here,' Monty muttered. 'That would make a real problem.'

Of course Sammy, the vagabond, had more sense than to wait about once he heard evidence of a human's approach. He snaked through the cat-flap next morning and hid under a hydrangea bush. The young girl neighbour who was looking after Monty arrived, suspecting nothing. Monty greeted her, tail aloft, in the kitchen. They made a fuss of each other. The girl opened another tin of meat and went to fetch Monty's bowl. In the sitting-room she paused. There was a strange smell there she didn't recognize. She looked all round for a clue to it, but found none.

'I'd better let some air in,' she said to Monty, who had followed her. She had the key to the patio door and so she unlocked it and slid it open. The fresh scents of the garden flooded into the room. Sammy watched everything tensely, ready to bolt. The girl seemed content to stand on the threshold and look out. The tabby was perfectly camouflaged against the thick dry stalks of the bush. The girl bent, picked up Monty's bowl and went back to the kitchen. Sammy remained motionless.

A whisper of a rustle behind him made him give a low growl. He was expecting more competition, but didn't turn his head. The next thing he knew Pinkie was beside him. She wasn't purring and made no attempt to nuzzle him.

'Human in the house,' he hissed sharply. 'She'll see you!' Sammy was only too aware that Pinkie's colouring could be picked out from a long way off.

His mate scuttled away to another part of the garden, but not before the girl in the kitchen had spied her. Suspecting immediately that the white cat was the cause

of the unfamiliar scent indoors, the girl ran round to
the open door, clapping her hands and calling, 'Shoo!
Go away! Shoo! Shoo!' The terrified Pinkie vanished.
Sammy, badly frightened himself, slunk deeper into the
bush, only just managing to stave off an instinctive desire
to flee. The girl, satisfied that she had rid the area of the
intruder, returned indoors and closed the patio door.
Minutes later she left the house and the coast was clear.
Sammy had survived.

Not until he was positive that there was no risk did
he stir and begin to call Pinkie. Monty came into the
garden.

'There's plenty left,' said the black cat. 'Enough for
two. The girl must think I'm a glutton.'

Sammy called Pinkie more urgently. She didn't answer
his calls and he grew more and more fretful. Then
hunger gripped him and took command. The food-bowl
beckoned. Before he could stop himself Sammy had
licked it clean. He looked at the empty bowl ruefully.
'Well, she couldn't have been hungry or she would have
come,' he muttered to himself by way of an excuse. But
he felt guilty and a cheat. 'I'll let her have all *my* share
next time,' he decided. 'That'll make it all right.'

But it wasn't all right. Pinkie had made a decision
herself. And that was to rely on her own hunting skills
and steer clear of anything to do with humans.

She recovered quickly from her fright once she was
on the other side of the high wall again. The gently
flowing river and the quietness of the towpath in the
early morning soothed her spirits. She roamed far along
the bank, content with her own company. Sammy's ideas
and hers seemed so far apart that she almost felt able
to put him out of her mind. She believed now that the
best way to avoid detection by the dreaded patrols was

to use the wit and cunning of the wild creature she really was. It simply wasn't possible for her to try to ape a pampered pet as Sammy had planned to do. Maybe he could succeed in that way. His kitten days had been spent in domesticity. But she knew she could never make a success of pretending to be a fireside pussy cat.

As Pinkie sought her prey the thought of Monty's meat – its smell, its taste – lingered in her mind. It wouldn't be easy to blot that out. A skinny mouse or two was a poor substitute. She hoped for something more sustaining.

A harsh voice suddenly interrupted her thoughts. 'Looking for grub?'

Pinkie swung round. Another white cat, hardly bigger than herself, was climbing up the bank from the river. It was as if she were looking at her double.

'I've just been having a drink,' the cat explained. 'Have you caught anything?'

'Er – not yet. Who are you?' Pinkie enquired.

'I could almost be your twin,' came the reply. 'Except I see you're older than I am.'

'I'm not that old,' Pinkie protested.

'No? Well, I'm the Pub Cat. They call me Snowy.'

'How original.'

'And you?'

'Pinkie.'

'Pinkie? Funny name for a white cat!'

'I'm pink underneath.'

'Very droll,' said Snowy. 'Look, that's where I live. Where my picture hangs over the path.'

Pinkie recognized the very spot where she and Sammy had escaped from the car. The building had a sign bracketed to the wall on the river side with a white cat painted on it. The sign swung slightly in the breeze.

Pinkie didn't know anything about pictures or pubs but she could see the image well enough.

'Why is that – that cat up there?' Pinkie faltered.

'That's me. I *am* the pub,' Snowy boasted. He really believed it. 'I mean, we're called the same.'

'Whatever are you saying? How can a human place be called Snowy?'

'No, no. Not Snowy,' he answered. '"The White Cat."'

'Oh.' Pinkie didn't understand at all.

'You look hungry,' said Snowy.

'I am.'

'Come with me, then.'

'No, I prefer to keep away from people. I don't trust humans.'

'Who said anything about humans? Though they're all right. Really.'

'Look,' said Pinkie. 'I have to catch something to eat. I can't waste any more time.'

'It's a hard life, scavenging, isn't it? I had to do a bit of it myself once. But since my pub days I –'

'I'm going,' Pinkie butted in. 'I can't just stand around here.'

'Have you ever tasted rabbit?'

Pinkie checked herself. 'Rabbit? Oh, yes.' Her mouth began to run water. She licked her chops. 'Not for ages, though.'

'OK. Now's your chance. Follow me.'

Snowy ran round the side of the building to the pub car park, which at that hour was empty. Across it was the pub garden and on the grass stood a large rabbit hutch. Two brown lop-eared rabbits were inside. Pinkie, having first made quite sure that no humans were around to bellow at her, trotted after Snowy.

'They're not rabbits,' she said.

'Certainly they are. Can't you smell them? And look at the meat on 'em!'

By now Pinkie had indeed recognized rabbit scent. 'They look different,' she murmured. 'But, yes . . .'

'Can you catch them?' Snowy cried. 'I've been trying for so long!'

Pinkie looked at him in bewilderment. 'You can't catch something in a cage,' she said.

'Can't you? I thought a wild, clever cat like you would find a way. You know – somehow get at them.'

Pinkie sauntered all around the hutch. The rabbits skittered nervously into their sleeping quarters. 'No. There's no way in there,' she announced. 'A dog might push this over, or dig underneath. And then . . .'

'A dog, yes,' said Snowy excitedly. 'Or a fox? I know a fox.'

'I wouldn't want any dealings with foxes. Such sly beasts. You couldn't trust a fox. And how do *you* know one?'

'Before I was the Pub Cat I was wild like you. I came across all kinds of creatures when I was hunting. The fox and I respected each other. We didn't interfere with each other's needs and co-operated to our mutual benefit. I still see him around sometimes on my wanderings, but he doesn't like to come close to humans.'

'I know the feeling,' Pinkie said. She was thinking hard. 'Where did you use to hunt?' she asked.

'Around the fields. Hedgerows, copses, that sort of thing. Most of them are gone now. Buildings instead.'

'Were there rabbits and so on?'

'Of course. Wild rabbits, squirrels, birds. It all seems a long time back. I've been claimed by the pub for two seasons.'

'And are there *any* fields left?'

'A few. Do you want to see them?' Snowy asked.

'I'd like to, yes.'

'All right. I'll take you there. And you'll help me with these bunnies here if we can get the fox to do a bit of digging?'

Pinkie had temporarily forgotten the lop-ears. She thought they were better left where they were. 'Well, yes, if we see the fox . . .' she replied vaguely.

'I'll see you later, then,' said Snowy. 'I've got to go and be the pub. People will be arriving soon.'

Pinkie moved away. 'Being the pub' was beyond her understanding. But she understood about people well enough and she didn't want any more scares. 'When shall I see you?' she asked.

'Stay along the riverside. I'll pick you up when I'm at liberty again.' Snowy ran off towards the pub's entrance, which was now open.

Pinkie went in the opposite direction. She hadn't caught anything and she was beginning to think of Monty's meat-bowl again.

The Church Cat

Word got around the local cat population of the fierce tabby who was hogging Monty's meat. As the news spread it was exaggerated and Sammy began to acquire the status of a kind of monster. A lot of curiosity was created and several of the cats were determined to go and see this phenomenon, so at dusk that day the inquisitive ones began to head for Monty's garden. One of these was a beautiful blue Persian who belonged to the local vicar and was referred to as the Church Cat by all the others. She was a magnificent specimen with long, silky blue-grey fur, coppery eyes, a proud expression, and a faultless pedigree. Her name was Hermione but no one called her that. She spent most of her time licking and polishing herself and kept apart from the others who she thought were mostly common and inferior. However, even she was interested in the existence of the 'bruiser' who had upset Domino so easily.

Sammy had spent most of the day in the garden. Every so often he called Pinkie but always in vain. Once or twice he climbed on to the high wall to look for her but she was nowhere to be seen. Sammy decided not to go any further than the wall. He didn't want to dirty his coat, which he was anxious to look after properly, as

Monty did his. And somehow the wall began to assume the nature of a boundary between his new regime of caring for himself like a pet and his old happy-go-lucky vagabond days.

'Where's your precious mate?' Monty dared to ask at one point as Sammy endlessly padded up and down.

'How should I know?' Sammy snapped back irritably. 'She was scared off, thanks to your human friend with the loud voice. She doesn't understand humans, Pinkie doesn't, not at all. There's nothing to be afraid of, if you're a pet.'

'But she's not a pet, is she?' Monty returned.

Sammy realized he had revealed more of his thoughts than he had intended. 'If she could behave like one, there would be no problem,' he said simply.

Monty looked long and hard at Sammy, expecting an explanation. None was forthcoming and he didn't have the courage to probe further.

'When will the girl come this evening?' Sammy asked, remembering his promise that Pinkie should have his share of the meat.

'That's all you care about – food – isn't it?' Monty was bold enough to comment. 'I told you before. Towards dusk. She wouldn't come in the dark. How long do you mean to stay here?'

Sammy stopped in his tracks. 'I've only just begun,' he answered. 'My plan's a long-term one. I want Pinkie and me to be safe like you. And we can be, both of us, if she'd only listen to my advice.'

'Safe?' Monty queried. 'Safe from what?'

'Danger. The round-up. The patrols. What do you think?' Sammy said in exasperation. He came close up to Monty who was resting in a sunny spot on the grass, his paws tucked under his chest. Sammy loomed over him. 'You've no complaints, have you?' he demanded.

'No, no, not at all, none that I can think of,' Monty answered hastily, jumping up and putting a distance between himself and the tabby. 'No,' he continued, 'you did what you said you would last time and I suppose –'

'I'll do it again, eh?' Sammy growled, half in jest. 'You bet I will. I'm a fixture here as far as any other cat is concerned. They'll soon appreciate that.' He grinned cocksurely. But Monty swallowed hard. He felt helpless. Only the return of his owners could alter that. And their return, he knew from experience, could be a long way off.

The inquisitive cats, among whom were Ling, Spike and the Church Cat, had all eaten their own meals during the day and, by the evening, were ready for a little excursion. Ling and Spike travelled together and arrived at the fence separating Monty's garden from the neighbour's. Timidly they waited a while before they climbed the final obstacle.

'It's quiet enough,' the grey Burmese said. 'Why don't you go and have a quick look over?'

'No, no, we'd better make sure we can't be seen first,' Spike answered at once. 'Is it *dark* enough?'

'Don't want it too dark or we won't see *it* – I mean him – will we?' Ling objected.

'Well, you go and look, then, if you're so keen,' the ginger said.

Ling's fat, eager face fell. 'All right, shall we go together?'

'Oh, come on, then. Ready? Up – we – go.'

They perched on top of the fence. At the other end of it a blue-grey shape loomed, teetering as it endeavoured to scan the ground.

'The Church Cat!' Ling hissed. 'What's *she* doing here?'

'The same as us, obviously,' Spike answered. 'Ah, hello, Monty.'

The black cat, whose food-bowl had become such a focal point, was sitting on his lawn, looking up at the gathering. 'No point in your coming,' he said irritably. 'I've a permanent guard in residence here. You haven't the remotest chance of getting anything to eat. In any case, you've no right to –'

'We haven't come for food,' Ling assured him. 'We heard about the – the – "guard",' she giggled. 'And we were curious.'

'Well, don't come any closer,' Monty warned. 'Sammy will think you're after his meat.'

'*His* meat?'

'It's mine really. You know that. But the tabby's laid claim to some of it. And what can I do? He's bigger than me and he's made my home his own. I'm no better off than before, when Domino and some of you lot used to come prowling around.'

Sammy hadn't touched the remnants of the latest food delivery. He had been saving it for Pinkie, who of course hadn't shown up. Now he heard the cats' voices and came to investigate. He saw Ling, Spike and the Church Cat on the fence and suspected a joint attack on the meat supply. More cats must be coming, he thought. Could he contain a whole mass of them? Better to eat the meat himself before he was overwhelmed. He growled fiercely at the onlookers, which was exactly what they had come to see, and raced for the cat-flap. It didn't take a minute for him to demolish the food.

'Phew!' Spike gasped. 'What a tiger! Rather your home than mine for that kind of companion.'

'You're such a comfort,' Monty said bitterly.

Sammy re-emerged. Now there was no possibility of a contest, he began to take an interest in the other cats. He looked admiringly at the Church Cat who was preening herself on the fence-top before leaving. Her curiosity had been satisfied.

'What a perfectly splendid coat you have,' Sammy said to her unexpectedly.

Hermione paused in her washing routine, one front paw left hanging in the air. 'One does one's best,' she mewed in a musical voice. 'It needs a lot of care and attention.'

'And apparently gets it,' Sammy remarked, adopting an indentical pose to the Persian's without realizing he was doing so.

The Church Cat fixed him with her copper-coloured eyes and then continued with her toilet, quite unconcerned. Ling and Spike were agog, wondering what would happen. Sammy watched Hermione avidly, then copied her movements with great precision. This was a wonderful opportunity for him to learn. The Church Cat, however, finished abruptly and jumped from the fence, out of view.

'Don't go!' Sammy called, bounding up the fence after her and putting to flight Ling and Spike as well as two other cats who had just arrived to take a peek at the monster. 'I want to know who you are. Where do you come from? I need you,' Sammy babbled, humbling himself before the Persian without a qualm.

'You need *me*?' she enquired haughtily. 'I hardly think we can have anything in common.' She stepped away daintily, wanting no truck with this savage.

'No, you see, I – what I meant was, I could be like you,' Sammy persisted, unconsciously aping her dainty walk.

The Church Cat turned and stared. 'I'm the Church Cat,' she announced. 'That tells you everything you need to know, I think. And I can assure you, you could *never* be anything like me.'

Sammy was heedless of the insult. He was spellbound by this superb creature – her superior air, her perfect deportment, her velvet fur. He followed her silently, trying to do everything the way she did it: every leap, every trot, every jump. Some of the other cats began to titter. The monster from Monty's garden now offered no more of a threat to them than a kitten following its mother. They laughed at the smitten tabby who ignored them, intent only on pursuing the beautiful blue Persian.

'Where's your tiger now?' Ling chortled as she and Spike went homewards.

'It's astonishing,' Spike replied. 'He seemed to change character completely. It makes me think Domino was fooled. That Sammy is all bluster.'

Hermione made her graceful way back to the vicarage, the last house in the row. She didn't understand why this rough, scarred tabby insisted on following her. She wanted nothing more to do with him. Sammy, on the other hand, had seen his ideal and was determined not to lose sight of it. If he could learn how to look as immaculate as this Persian, he need never fear a patrol swoop again. And, of course, what he learnt would be passed on to Pinkie as well. At the entrance to the vicarage the Church Cat turned.

'I hope you're not coming for my food,' she trilled. 'You'll get none here.'

'Food?' muttered Sammy. 'I've *had* food. I want to watch you.'

The Church Cat blinked and stretched her legs elaborately. Sammy did the same. Hermione shook her hind legs, one after the other, and ambled up the path to the front of the house. Sammy shook his hind legs and ambled after her. A security light flashed on as the Persian jumped up to a front window sill.

'That's my signal,' she told Sammy. 'I'll be let in now. There's no convenient little door here for intruders to use. So you'll simply *have* to go away.' She drawled the last sentence in a very affected manner.

'. . . *have* to go away. *Have* to go away,' Sammy echoed, practising the Church Cat's accent.

'Stupid creature,' Hermione murmured as a window opened and she whisked inside.

Sammy sat and gazed after her. For a long time he waited, hoping for another glimpse of this perfect model. He was disappointed and, finally, he stirred. '*Have* to go away. *Have* to go away. I *have* to go away,' he mimicked dreamily. Without thinking about where he was going he wandered into the churchyard, still trying to move in that easy, graceful style that had so entranced him. He had forgotten all about Pinkie. Beyond the churchyard there was a low stone wall. Sammy noticed a white cat vault over it and vanish into the darkness. His mate's brief appearance was a shock and he suddenly came to himself.

'Pinkie!' he called. 'Over here. It's me!' She didn't materialize and he ran to the wall and jumped on to it. There was a field on the other side in which were rows of tombstones. It was used for burials now that the original graveyard was full. It was mostly unkempt, although there were areas where some people had kept their relatives' graves tidy. In one of these clearings Sammy saw Pinkie devouring a kill. His feelings of guilt returned.

'Have you had luck?' he cried, running up. He saw her prey was only a vole.

'Can you call this luck?' she snapped. 'All day I've been out and around hunting and this and a dead mouse are all I've come up with.'

Sammy's face dropped. How he regretted breaking

his vow. 'You – you could have all the meat *next* time,' he said in a small voice. It always seemed to be 'next time'.

Pinkie's resolve had weakened. Her stomach was hollow and she craved a good meal. 'I'll come now,' she said. 'Just to eat. I won't stay. Is it safe?'

'Yes. It's safe. But – well, I had to eat the food this time. There's no more till the morning.'

Pinkie stared at him. She understood. 'Your greed got the better of you,' she summed up. 'How do I know that won't happen again?'

'I promise,' said Sammy. And he did mean it. 'Come early tomorrow. I'll be waiting indoors with Monty. And, Pinkie, try to clean yourself up a bit in the meantime. Your coat is horribly soiled and you smell a bit rank. You don't seem to be looking after yourself at all.'

—9—

The fox

During that day Pinkie had rambled up and down the riverside, wondering when the Pub Cat would be released to join her. She had high hopes of the rabbit hunt. It was late in the afternoon when Snowy at last came into view from the pub end of the towpath. Pinkie was so eager to begin she rushed up to him.

'I'm starving,' she said. 'I've only made one catch so far. There was a dead mouse by the wall but I hardly touched it because I knew there'd be better prey later.'

Snowy looked puzzled. 'Better prey? Where?'

'*I* don't know,' Pinkie answered testily. 'You're going to show me, aren't you? Wild rabbits, you said, and a – a fox to help us.' She hoped Snowy wouldn't remember his plan to ensnare the lop-eared bunnies.

'Oh, that,' Snowy muttered. 'I'd forgotten. Yes, all right then. You'd better follow me. We go this way.' He led off down the path in the direction of the church. Eventually they passed the church wall, after several diversions caused by Pinkie's need to hide from human strollers. The field with its gravestones yielded nothing in the way of quarry at that point. 'We'll have to wait and see if the fox turns up,' Snowy advised. 'He'll know where to go.'

'But I thought you knew where to go?' Pinkie complained.

'Places change a lot,' Snowy excused himself. 'The
last time I saw the fox was in this field. At one time it
was all open country from here to – to – well, as far as
a cat could go.'

'Let's go further, then.'

'I wouldn't like to risk it without the fox. I'm not sure
what we might find. People and buildings, possibly. You
wouldn't like that. But the fox would know.'

'So where does he come from, then?' Pinkie demanded
crossly. 'There must be somewhere suitable farther on.
A fox doesn't make his home amongst humans.'

'Hm. I don't know about that. These days it's different. They're bolder than they were, foxes,' Snowy
waffled.

'Oh, this is no good at all,' Pinkie cried. 'I think you've
led me on. I don't believe in this fox!'

'You'll believe when you see him,' Snowy assured
her.

'And what if I don't see him?'

'Then you must come again another day. He'll show
some time.'

While the Pub Cat amused himself by alternately
dozing on a warm gravestone and chasing early but-
terflies, Pinkie watched and waited for an animal who
she now only half believed existed. After a while she
lost interest and began to search for prey. Suddenly
she sensed that she was being observed, and looked
about her. The Pub Cat was asleep. Then she saw
the fox, or what could be described as the shadow of
one. A skinny, moth-eaten-looking creature was limping
across the field, staring directly at her. The fox's tail had
lost most of its fur and he had an ear missing. Pinkie
remained still. Was this the fox the Pub Cat thought

could undermine the lop-ears' hutch? Surely not. This one would hardly have the strength to walk the distance required.

'Snowy!' Pinkie hissed. 'Is this your fox?'

Snowy's eyes blinked open and he got up. 'Oh, *there* he is. Yes, that's him. He doesn't seem to be wearing well, does he?'

'I think he's on his last legs,' Pinkie remarked scornfully. 'What use can he be?'

There wasn't time for an answer. The fox came up, panting. 'Anything to eat?' he gasped, without acknowledging the Pub Cat in any way. 'I'm famished.'

Pinkie was too stunned to respond.

'Have you found anything? Can you spare me a bit of it?' the pathetic creature continued.

'Like a rabbit, you mean?' Pinkie asked sarcastically.

'Oh, yes. Yes. Have you caught one? Oh, wonderful. Where is it?'

'She's pulling your leg,' Snowy told the fox.

'Oh. Oh, don't do that – it might come off,' the creature joked feebly. 'I'm sure bits of me are falling off all the time. Oh, how I'd love some rabbit. I can't catch them any more.'

Pinkie's ears pricked up. At least this sounded as though there were still some around. 'You don't look as if you could catch *anything* much,' she observed critically.

'No. Only diseases,' the fox quipped hollowly. 'So you've nothing for me, then? Oh dear.'

'You've fallen on hard times, Fox,' Snowy said. 'You don't look well at all.'

'How could I? I haven't eaten a thing for days except berries. And they were rotten.'

'If you show us where the rabbits are, perhaps *we* could catch one,' Pinkie said. 'And you could share.'

'Oh no. Don't make me go all the way back, 'the fox pleaded. 'I'm exhausted already. You sure you haven't got *something* here?'

'Nothing,' Pinkie insisted. 'And how did you know you'd find anyone here?'

The fox glanced at her with dull eyes. 'I didn't. I was searching for scraps. When I saw a white cat my spirits lifted. I was hopeful.'

'He remembers me, you see,' the Pub Cat explained.

The fox turned his gaze on Snowy. 'You can't help me any more than she can, I suppose?' he muttered.

'We can help each other,' Snowy replied eagerly. 'There are two fat rabbits in a box and we –'

'Don't waste your breath,' Pinkie cut in. 'Look at him. What possible help could he be?'

The fox turned slowly and, with the remants of his tail between his legs, hobbled abjectly away. He had gained nothing from the cats except insults. Pinkie felt some regret. She ran after the animal.

'If you take me where the wild rabbits are, I *will* help you,' she offered. 'I'm sorry for what I said. It was cruel of me.'

The skinny fox was so tired and worn out that he had to lie down. 'Haven't got enough energy to breathe hardly,' he croaked. 'Bring me a morsel of something – anything – to give me a wisp of strength and I'll try. But not now. I've got to rest first.'

'I'll see what I can find,' Pinkie said. She returned to the Pub Cat. 'He's done for if he doesn't eat soon. I'll try to rake something up for him. What about you?'

'Me? I'm not a hunter, you know. Not any more. Used to be before I became the pub. But now – no, I wouldn't be any good. Lost the knack, I expect.'

'I shouldn't wait then,' Pinkie said sharply. 'I'll do what I can. Leave the fox to me.'

'By all means,' replied the Pub Cat. 'I oughtn't to stay away too long anyhow. The White Cat sign says I'm there. But I'm not at the moment.'

Snowy's gobbledygook was lost on Pinkie. She remembered the dead mouse she had left. That would be a start. She quickly fetched it and the fox was delighted with the poor scrap. He swallowed it almost without chewing.

'Of course when you have such a great hunger, something like that can irritate rather than help,' Pinkie mentioned. 'I'm sorry there is nothing more substantial.'

The fox gulped twice, easing the passage of the carrion. 'Don't knock it,' he wheezed. 'It's as good as a day's supply of food for a creature like me.'

Pinkie looked sympathetically at this poor bag of bones. 'You can't survive on that,' she said. 'When did you last eat properly?'

The fox grinned, showing almost toothless jaws. 'When I last had all my teeth,' he joked. 'It's not easy to eat properly without them.'

'Very comical,' Pinkie observed drily. 'I wonder you can carry on like that.'

The fox seemed about to go to sleep. He yawned and panted, 'It's the only way to fight misfortune.'

'There's another way,' Pinkie said quickly. She was still thinking of a rabbit hunt. 'Look for help.'

'I always do,' the fox murmured. 'And I'm always disappointed.' He closed his eyes and tried to settle himself more comfortably.

'You won't sleep out here in the open, surely?' Pinkie said. 'What about humans? Dogs? There's a big Alsatian living not far away.'

The fox opened one eye to look at Pinkie. 'Don't worry about this battered beast,' he advised. 'They all pass me by. I look as though I'm dead.'

Pinkie was moved to pity by the fox's resignation. She decided to stay with him for a while, despite his almost overpowering smell. She hoped that later he might recover sufficiently to show her the hunting area. Meanwhile she felt she wanted to stay on guard. The fox lay perfectly still and certainly didn't appear even to be breathing. But now and then one of his limbs would twitch, showing unmistakably that he was still alive.

Pinkie watched over him for a spell. She was content to clean her whiskers and wait. No one came into the field. The fox showed no sign of stirring and, eventually, Pinkie had to think again about prey. If not rabbit today, at least something must be caught. She couldn't fast any longer. She roamed the field, glancing across now and then at the sleeping animal. She mistimed a pounce and allowed a blackbird to escape her claws. The bird flew off, shrieking alarm and waking the fox who slowly and laboriously hoisted himself to his feet. Pinkie's eyes followed the flight of the blackbird in disgust. She didn't see the old fox slink away.

When Sammy found her she had given up all hope of finding the fox again. She sought him everywhere, as far as a fringe of trees on the farther side of the field. He had disappeared, much to her regret. The wizened beast had strangely affected Pinkie with his matter-of-fact acceptance of his thread of a life. Moreover his absence removed the key to the possible rabbit chase. Pinkie longed for his return and somehow the arrival of Sammy irritated her. The tabby's demeanour seemed so smug and complacent by comparison. How typical that he had eaten all the available meat without a second thought! *He* had never been reduced to eating the remnants of a mouse carcass in order to survive one more day. Of course Pinkie's memory was at fault. Sammy had suffered great hardship in his younger vagabond days in Quartermile Field. But that was all a long time ago.

After Sammy left, the little white cat napped the remainder of the night, waking every so often with the memory of her mate's critical remarks about her appearance and smell. Some of the fox's odour, she knew, must cling to her fur. She couldn't do anything about that. But in the morning she did make a half-hearted effort to lick herself clean before setting off for Monty's garden, wary but determined this time to fill her stomach. She reached the top of the high wall and waited. It was still early. Pinkie had no way of knowing if the meat was in the house or not. She wondered if Sammy would notice she had cleaned herself up. She was annoyed with herself for feeling any concern about it, but somehow his words had made her a little self-conscious.

After a while she saw Monty's head peep through the cat-flap. Sammy had instructed the black cat to look out for her. Monty saw her immediately and trotted towards her. Pinkie recognized his gleaming black coat, shining with health and, she imagined, combed and perfumed by a careful human owner. She looked down at herself. Specks of mud, burrs, and strands of dead grass decorated her chest fur. She pawed hastily at it as Monty ran up.

'Hurry up and come,' the black cat invited her. 'Sammy won't wait for ever. He stood over me while I ate. I hardly dared to swallow more than a few mouthfuls. I'm sure he would have driven me away from my bowl if I'd eaten more than he thought I should. He said he wanted to save as much as he could for you. As much as *he* could! As though the meat's more his than mine now. He has no right to –'

'I'll come at once,' Pinkie interrupted, jumping down

from the wall. 'I do need that meat. Has the human who shouted at me disappeared?'

'Oh yes. But I don't know how long Sammy can stay in my home without being discovered. He sees it as his own place now. He hardly bothers to hide himself when the girl comes. One of these days he's going to take one risk too many and that can't come soon enough for me.'

Pinkie had some sympathy with Monty whose den and food had been all but usurped by the bullying Sammy. However, she didn't comment, because without Sammy there would be no meat for her now.

She miaowed a friendly greeting as she reached Monty's personal door. Sammy miaowed back with genuine pleasure.

'You came. I'm so glad,' he said. 'Tuck in, Pinkie. I've denied myself even a single mouthful.' He wasn't quite so glad when Pinkie stepped through the cat-flap into what had become his sleeping quarters.

'Humph!' Sammy sniffed at her. 'You won't be able to remain here long, you know, tainting the air. Wherever did you get that dreadful smell from?'

Pinkie turned to glance at him but continued to chew. The meat was rich and moist and succulent. She savoured its taste on her tongue.

'Pinkie?' Sammy cried. He wanted an answer.

'I spent some time with a fox,' she mumbled. 'I suppose I picked up some of his –'

'A fox!' Sammy bellowed. 'What on earth are you up to, Pinkie? Pets don't mingle with wild animals. They prefer to keep themselves clean,' he added pointedly. 'Look at the state of you! How do you think you're helping yourself by consorting with foxes?'

'There was a chance he might have led me to some real food,' Pinkie explained.

'You've got food,' Sammy retorted angrily. 'Proper

food that pet cats eat, which will make you look more like one yourself. Can't you see how much good it's doing *me*?' He exhibited himself, stepping haughtily around her as he had seen the Church Cat do. Pinkie watched him wonderingly.

'You're certainly beginning to look sleeker,' she admitted, before turning again to the meat. 'But why are you parading around like that?'

'It's all part of pet behaviour,' Sammy replied excitedly. 'I've seen the perfect pet. She sets the most marvellous example. We couldn't hope for a better teacher.'

'Teacher?' snapped Pinkie jealously. 'What other tricks is she putting you up to?'

'None. She's quite disdainful of me,' Sammy told her honestly. 'I know I haven't learnt enough yet. She told me to go away. "You'll *have* to go away." ' Sammy copied Hermione's accent faithfully. 'That's how she sounds,' he continued. 'Wonderful, isn't it? And when you and I can look and talk like her she'll accept us. That's our goal, Pinkie. Because when the Church Cat accepts us, we'll have achieved our aim.'

Pinkie had paused again during this strange outpouring. She thought Sammy had taken leave of his senses. 'Aim?' she echoed. 'What aim?'

'To be perfect pets, of course, like her,' Sammy answered irritably. 'Haven't you listened to me at all?'

'I see,' Pinkie whispered. Her tail twitched ominously. She was angry. 'Well, you may want to go mincing around like this – this Church Cat,' she spat, 'but you can tell her she can forget about *my* education. I've no wish to be taught by anyone! I'll make my own way and that's the best way for *me*!'

Now Sammy was angry. 'Oh, you know everything, of course, don't you? Including, I suppose, how to evade capture? Good. Well, *don't* listen to me. My ideas are

obviously of no use to you. So you can leave the rest of
that to me!' He pushed Pinkie roughly from the food-
bowl and gobbled down what was left of the meat.

'You're making a fool of yourself,' was Pinkie's last
retort. 'And you don't realize it!'

'Go away,' Sammy hissed. 'And don't come back
again while you smell like that.'

'Oh, I *have* to go away,' crooned Pinkie, sarcastically
aping Sammy's idol, which made him even more furious,
so that he almost chased her from the garden. But Pinkie
wasn't frightened of her mate and had the last laugh.
From the top of the high wall she taunted him.

'I *have* to go away. He doesn't like my smell. I *have*
to go away.'

Past and present

Monty witnessed the cats' quarrel from the fence-top. He could tell there was some trouble but, naturally, didn't understand the cause.

'She'll see,' Sammy vowed bitterly. 'She'll find out the hard way.' He slunk to the shade of a tall plant and flung himself down. Pinkie's words had upset him more than he cared to admit.

And Pinkie, too, was far from happy. When she jumped from the wall she realized she had put a barrier between herself and Sammy. The upshot of their disagreement was that she couldn't return to the house to feed again. Moreover she was jealous. The Church Cat, Sammy's ideal, had become more important to him than his mate.

'I thought he had more sense,' she muttered to herself. 'He's blinded. Neither of us can ever be like her.' She sauntered along, then stopped suddenly. Where was she going? She didn't know any more. 'Oh, now what do I do?' she wailed. 'I don't have a den and I don't have a mate any longer. Sammy has a base but I don't have anything. Where would I hide from the patrols?'

The more she thought about her predicament the more Pinkie realized that there was only one creature who knew a sufficiently wide area to be able to help her. And that was the fox. The poor toothless, decrepit creature had once been a clever, resourceful hunter with all the skills and knowledge necessary to thrive. He would still be familiar with the safest places and he could surely give her guidance.

'Where would he have gone and will he have survived?' Pinkie asked herself. 'I must find him quickly.' She ran to the churchyard and was about to leap the low stone wall into the field with the gravestones when the presence of another cat, a beautiful blue Persian sitting further along the wall, made her hesitate. At first the Church Cat pretended not to notice Pinkie although she was looking directly across. She yawned and stretched thoroughly, then gave Pinkie a kind of dismissive glance as if to convey her complete lack of interest and stepped daintily along the wall, turning her back on the white cat. Pinkie concluded at once who the animal was and she felt bitter. Here was the creature Sammy wished her to emulate; a proud, vain-looking beast who hadn't even the courtesy to acknowledge her presence.

'I'd rather be the ruffian I am,' Pinkie swore as she jumped hastily over the wall.

The fox wasn't in the field. This time Pinkie went beyond the fringe of trees and entered a small copse. It wasn't long before she detected the fox's scent.

'He must be here somewhere,' she told herself. 'He was too weak to travel further.'

She found the fox under a hawthorn tree. He was lying on his back, his body slightly twisted and completely still. Pinkie was quite sure she was too late and miaowed her frustration and disappointment. Amazingly the fox stirred, righted himself with a wriggle and sat up.

'I – I thought . . .' Pinkie stammered.

'I was playing dead. Not a difficult act for me!' the fox said. 'A man brought a big dog in here and I didn't have a den to escape to. It was all I could think of when the great brute came bounding up.'

'What happened?'

'It sniffed at me and ran on past. I'm not of much interest to anybody.'

'You are to me,' Pinkie told him.

The fox grinned. 'Are you still thinking of those rabbits?'

'No. I'm not hungry right now. But I want your help in another way.'

'Yes, there's the smell of good meat on your breath,' the fox commented. He gave a croak of amusement. 'I suppose that's the closest I'll get to tasting it. Unless you can tell me where to find some?'

Pinkie had to put him off this track pretty swiftly. 'Er – no. It wouldn't be possible for you. It was pet food. But look, have you eaten anything since that mouse I found you?'

'A few beetles and slugs. Not much meat on any of 'em.'

'The Pub Cat used to hunt with you, didn't he? Long ago? I could take his place. I'm fast. I can catch things. Perhaps I can be of benefit to you? But I need a proper den. Somewhere secure. You can help *me* there.'

'Look at me. Do you really think so?' the fox said ironically. 'You're kidding yourself. And what's the Pub Cat?'

'The white cat – Snowy. He knows you from way back, doesn't he?'

'Maybe. I don't remember much. My wits have gone.'

'Nonsense. You still know what's what,' Pinkie said. 'Don't you have a den?'

'Not a proper one. Best I can do is a hollow under a rock.'

'It doesn't sound very comfortable.'

'It isn't. It gets flooded when the river's high,' the fox replied. 'But no other creature uses it or knows of it.'

'I'm not surprised,' Pinkie said bluntly. 'Then it's on the river bank?'

'Beyond the bridge. That's where the rabbits are.'

Pinkie's ears pricked up. This would be useful for the future. 'When you're ready to move,' she said, 'I'll come with you. Maybe I'll find a place to make my own den on the way.'

'I'm too tired to move,' the fox said. 'I'll be all right here. I don't ask for much, or expect it these days.' He lay down and wrapped his scanty brush around his nose. 'If you spy an earwig or a moth anywhere,' he muttered sardonically, 'let me know. I might just be able to catch it.'

Pinkie saw that the emaciated beast was ready for sleep. She left the fox where he lay and began to prowl around the copse. Under a pine tree a pigeon fledgeling flapped helplessly, having fallen from its nest. Pinkie pounced and carried its lifeless body, dangling in her jaws, to the slumbering fox.

'Have that on me when you wake,' she murmured. 'Perhaps it'll give you the strength to take me where I want to go.'

The rest of the copse yielded nothing. Pinkie found a warm tree-stump in the full rays of the sun and settled herself on it for a snooze. She contemplated the scarcity of food for a fox who could no longer hunt and wondered how he had survived the winter. 'Beetles, berries and a flooded den,' she mused. 'What a life! Is that what I'm heading for?'

*   *   *

Not far away, in Monty's garden, Sammy was basking lazily. He had scarcely given a thought to Pinkie except to wonder what she would do. He had been grilling Monty about the Church Cat. He wanted to know everything about her. Monty was able to tell him very little and Sammy was all the more in awe of Hermione because of her mystery.

'Why are you so interested?' Monty asked him. As a house cat himself, the distinction between his and the Church Cat's way of life was negligible. There was no contrast as there was with Sammy's.

'She's the perfect pet,' the tabby answered him. 'She thinks I'm a tramp but I can learn.'

'Learn what?' Monty enquired in a puzzled voice.

'To do as you do. Look!' Sammy cried, jumping up and stalking in front of the black cat. 'Don't you think my fur is glossier? I'm being much more careful about it. And my walk's not so stiff, is it? I don't look so much like the typical old tom when I move. I sway more, I'm more – er – nonchalant.'

'Yes. Yes, I see,' Monty responded awkwardly. 'Very good. You're softening up, you mean?'

Sammy's attitude changed at once. 'No, I'm not softening up,' he growled, pushing his face close to Monty's. 'Don't you believe it. Any cat who thinks so is in for a surprise! I'm learning tricks, that's what I'm doing. Tricks to trick the humans with.'

Monty backed away. The tiger in Sammy still lurked just beneath the surface. The black cat didn't understand this strange animal and bemoaned the absence of his owners and the existence of his little cat-door that had brought Sammy so abruptly and disturbingly into his life.

After the evening feed, which Sammy had no qualms

about finishing, the tabby set off to add to his education.
Monty, because of Sammy's looming presence, was
eating far less than he should and was beginning to
lose weight. Sammy, of course, didn't notice. *He* had
never been so well fed and didn't stop to think about
fair shares.

A gentle drizzle was falling as he headed in the
direction of the vicarage, practising his new walk as
he went. On the way he saw no other cats. Perhaps
the rain was keeping them indoors. Sammy, used to all
kinds of weather, relished the freshness of the evening
and all the scents that were heightened by the cool
atmosphere. At the vicarage the Church Cat was sitting
by an open window on the inside sill, watching the rain
with a passive expression.

Sammy sat on his haunches and looked at her. Would
she come out or would the dampness prevent her?
Did pets shun wet weather? Should he have stayed
indoors? 'She'll know the right thing to do, anyway,'
Sammy thought to himself. 'I can learn from this.'

A drop of rain splashed one of Hermione's paws
as she sat looking out of the window. She lifted the
paw daintily and gave it a little shake as if to rid
herself of the unpleasant feeling. Sammy, who by this
time was wet all over, absorbed this piece of fussiness
greedily. He lifted up a front paw, gave it a shake,
then did the same with the other. Then he stood up
and repeated the process with his hind feet. Finally
he gave his entire coat a vigorous shake, calculating
that had Hermione been as wet as he was she would
have done the same.

Still the Church Cat was content to sit. Sammy grew
a little bored. 'Are you coming out?' he called. 'Or –
or – isn't that done?'

The Persian's eyes sought the source of the voice.

Sammy walked forward. 'Here I am,' he said. 'It's me again.'

'So I see,' the Church Cat remarked without pleasure. 'What are you doing in my garden?'

'Waiting for you,' Sammy replied hopefully.

'Then you'll have a long wait. I don't mix with your sort.'

Sammy was chastened. He realized he didn't yet reach the required standard. Then he thought of something. 'You came to see *me*,' he reminded the haughty creature.

'I heard tales,' she answered, 'and took a look for myself. Seeing is one thing; mixing with, quite another.'

'Well,' Sammy prompted eagerly, 'what did you think of me?'

'I saw what I thought I would see,' the Church Cat answered lazily. 'A tough street fighter.'

Sammy wasn't sure whether to be flattered by this image of himself. 'I'm not that much of a fighter,' he told her. 'I was just guarding my interests.'

'*Your* interests?' the Church Cat drawled. 'In another cat's garden?'

'My garden, too, now,' Sammy assured her stiffly. 'I've won the right to be there.'

The Persian was becoming more attentive, despite herself. 'But you don't come from round here?' she murmured. 'You seem to have arrived suddenly?'

Sammy didn't reply at once. Here was a chance for him to raise himself in the Church Cat's estimation. His vagabond days in the park were in the past. No need to refer to them at all. He could be any cat he chose to be in this new way of life. No one would ever know, except Pinkie, and she was unlikely to put in an appearance.

'I lost my mistress,' he said. 'She died. So there was nobody to look after me. I became homeless and uncared for. I had to feed myself. I joined a group of – um – other homeless creatures and learnt how to hunt. I became the best hunter; better than any of them. I was the King Cat.' He paused to see if the title impressed Hermione. She was standing now, half in and half out of the window. She seemed to have forgotten the drizzle.

Sammy continued, 'But I always longed for those comforts again. I moved around, rambling here and there, hoping for a kind word, a loving hand, real food, warmth and comfort. I couldn't seem to find any of those things.'

'What a sad story,' the Church Cat whispered. 'I'd no idea.'

Sammy warmed to his theme. 'The more I had to roam, the wilder I must have appeared. Small wonder I couldn't attract human compassion. So you can understand how thankful I was to accept Monty's offer.'

'His – offer?' the Church Cat murmured.

'Yes. Food and shelter in return for keeping intruders away. At last I have some of the home comforts back again. I feel a new animal and I try, with each day, to become like the happy house pet I used to be with my dear mistress.'

Hermione jumped into the garden and came towards him. 'You said you needed me,' she said archly, 'that time you followed me home. I didn't understand before. You meant I could help you to – to become civilized again?'

'That's it exactly,' Sammy concurred enthusiastically. 'You set me the most perfect example. Of course I could never hope to acquire your elegance.'

The Persian actually began to purr. 'Well,' she said, 'the King Cat hasn't forgotten how to pass a compliment. Perhaps it won't be so difficult to help rid him of a few rough edges.'

——11——

Rabbit search

When the fox awoke in the copse he couldn't believe his eyes. There was no sign of Pinkie so he didn't connect the pigeon fledgeling with her in any way. This carrion was pure bounty for him. His few remaining teeth were soon tearing off the flimsy feathers. There wasn't a lot of meat, but for the old fox it was a feast. He smacked his lips over it.

Pinkie returned and feigned surprise. 'Has it revived you?' she asked.

'Yes,' the fox wheezed. 'For a few moments longer!'

'Perhaps your luck's changed,' said Pinkie. 'How do you feel about hunting rabbit?'

'Embittered,' the fox replied. 'You keep talking of it and you know I'm incapable.'

'*Show* me the rabbits,' Pinkie pleaded. 'Give me a chance.'

'I'll show you, I'll show you,' the fox declared. 'And then will you stop goading?'

'I never meant to be –'

'Come on!' the old fox snapped. 'You have to catch me when I'm mobile.' And off he went, half limping, half trotting, through the copse to the riverside. The railway bridge straddled the river a short distance ahead. The fox avoided the towpath, which skirted one of the bridge's great iron supporting pillars, and continued along the bank itself.

'Is that your den?' Pinkie cried, seeing a dark muddy entrance hole under a lump of sandstone.

The fox paused and turned. He had been about to go on past. 'Yes, that's home,' he panted. 'Cosy, isn't it?' He gave Pinkie a sarcastic grin.

The little white cat almost shuddered. 'There must be . . . somewhere better than this,' she whispered.

'Find it, then!' was the response.

Pinkie looked back at the black mass of the bridge. Just then a train began to rumble across from the opposite side of the river. The rumble became thunder as it approached. The ground on which the animals stood vibrated. Pinkie thought the earth was going to open up and she raced away.

'Nothing comforting for a creature around here,' the fox growled, bowing his bony body against the deafening noise. When the train had passed over he hobbled after the frightened cat. 'That'll have scattered the rabbits,' he muttered, 'if there ever were any.'

'How can you live under the path of that . . . that . . . monstrous caterpillar?' Pinkie demanded.

'I don't live,' the fox grunted. 'I exist. And barely that.'

'Do you sleep in that black place?'

'Sometimes. If the river's low like it is now. But if it rains heavily I usually steer clear of it.'

'Where do you go then?'

'Anywhere. I have no other den. Look around you. Do you see any scope?'

Pinkie had already noticed the dearth of shelter. The ground was bare and open. A drainage ditch ran across it and emptied its contents into the river. The ditch was too wide for the fox to jump and therefore marked the extent of his territory. Away from the river, beyond the open ground, were more buildings comprising a small industrial development.

'This is where you'll find rabbits,' the fox said abruptly as he saw Pinkie's blank look.

She had almost forgotten them. 'Where?'

'By the ditch. They like to nibble the young spring growth alongside. And they use it to drink from when they can. Their homes are in the river bank beyond it.'

'I don't see any now.'

'Well, you wouldn't. There's not much for them to eat there at present. Too early in the season. And if there *had* been any, the train would have made them bolt.'

Pinkie was scanning the river bank where the fox had said the timid creatures had their warren. There was no sign of life. Indeed the entire area had a distinctly desolate look about it. She wondered where on earth she would find shelter when she needed it without risking a return to the environment of humans. She wandered to the edge of the ditch and looked across. It would require a mighty big leap to get to the other side. She glanced at the muddy water flowing along the ditch bottom, then turned her back. There would be no rabbit hunting. The image of Monty's food-bowl seemed to flash across all this emptiness like a beacon. But Pinkie was determined not to give in yet.

'Does the ditch ever run dry?' she asked the fox.

'Maybe, if the rabbits are particularly thirsty,' the ragged beast quipped. 'Oh,' he chuckled, 'I see your drift. You're really hooked on this rabbit round-up, aren't you? Well, I told you. *I* can't catch them.'

Pinkie's thoughts took flight as soon as she heard the word 'round-up'. She was back with Sammy and their poor lost kittens in the park. She heard again the tramp of heavy boots and, in a panic of realization, saw herself as she would be seen now on this barren and muddy piece of land by those fierce, eager humans. She began to tremble as if their nets had already trapped her, as if their hands already grasped her. She remembered Sammy's gibe. No, of course she didn't know how to evade capture, except by running . . . She broke there and then into a half-run and only the fox's croaky voice brought her back to reality.

'Where are you going now?'

Pinkie came to an abrupt halt. She blinked at the fox dumbly. 'I – I don't know. I need shelter,' she mumbled.

'Well, you'd better come with me. I'm going to my den. Nothing doing here.' The fox limped away.

'Huh! I'm not that desperate for shelter,' Pinkie whispered with the ghost of a grin. 'I'd sooner be up a tree.' However, her sympathies were aroused again as she watched the decrepit fox slink towards the one place in the whole hostile neighbourhood he could call home. 'Poor creature,' she mewed. 'Life *has* treated him badly.' She recalled that the Pub Cat had known him in the past, and wondered what he had been like when he was young. She crept after him, ready to flee from the slightest sound on the railway bridge.

The fox's earthy den smelt even more strongly than the animal himself. From this Pinkie guessed that the river water hadn't recently paid a visit to wash the place clean. She peered under the boulder into the gloom. Inside the den was as dark as night. The fox's muffled voice reached her.

'Come inside if you wish. It's dry enough.'

Pinkie hesitated, her nose a-quiver. In the end her natural inquisitiveness got the better of her and she stepped inside. Her pupils dilated enormously. The place had some kind of lining – dead vegetation, flotsam

left by the river's penetration and now merely damp –
which added to the den's dank scent.

'Not a particularly fragrant spot, is it?' the cat commented.

There came a hollow laugh. 'I don't worry about
smells,' the fox said. 'It's wondering about the taste
of things that concerns me.'

'Like rabbit?'

'No. I *know* the taste of rabbit.'

'So you have caught them?'

'Of course. When I was young and nimble.'

'You haven't eaten well for a while, have you?'

The fox gave no answer save for a deep sigh.

'There must be some way to get at those creatures,'
Pinkie muttered. 'If only Sammy were here. What a
rabbit hunter he used to be!'

The fox was silent. He was dreadfully weary and had
fallen asleep. Pinkie left him, full of the idea of enlisting
Sammy's help. However, she wasn't very confident of
success. He had altered so much.

'I'll appeal to his hunting instincts,' she told herself.
'He can't have lost all his old dash.'

Outside the musky den Pinkie looked toward the
open ground. 'The copse is the only place for me,' she
decided. 'I'll have to sleep in a tree. There's nothing
over there except – what's that?' she suddenly hissed.
There was movement in several places on the bare,
broken ground. Rabbits! There were burrow entrances
here which the fox didn't know about. It hardly seemed
possible, but rabbits were popping up and scampering
towards the ditch on *this* side.

Pinkie flattened herself. The rabbits were unaware of
her presence. She crept forward on her belly. 'The fox
must be blind!' she whispered. Another rabbit emerged,
its back to Pinkie, but almost under her nose. She leapt

forward and somehow managed to pin it to the ground, although it wasn't much smaller than she. Pinkie held on desperately, using her teeth and claws until her prey was exhausted. Then she dragged it, bumping over the uneven ground, until she reached the fox's den again.

'Fox! Look! A banquet!' Pinkie panted triumphantly.

The fox was on his feet. 'What did you . . . ? Where did you . . . ?' he spluttered.

'Never mind now. Eat.'

The fox tore into the rabbit hide with his front claws; his few teeth were of no use here. 'There's more meat on this than *I* can eat,' he asserted. 'The spoils should go to the hunter.'

'I'll take my share later,' said Pinkie. 'Listen, there are more of these for the taking. On *this* side of the ditch. Didn't you know that?'

The fox was busy with his eating for some while. Eating was a long-winded business for him because it was so difficult to chew. At last he said, 'My sight's not so good. It's failing, like the rest of me. I might see things without realizing it. But you can do well here.'

'Not on my own,' Pinkie replied. 'I was lucky this time. It needs teamwork.'

The fox gave a wheezy chuckle. 'Teamwork? Then don't think of *me*. What good would I be?'

Pinkie kept quiet. She had been thinking again of begging Sammy to join her.

After eating a few mouthfuls off the carcass, Pinkie spent the night in the copse, moving restlessly from tree to tree, from branch to branch. There was nowhere very suitable for a cat to sleep. The contrast between her wild existence and Sammy's adopted one was now so marked that Pinkie was in two minds whether to attempt to approach her one-time mate.

'I'll try once more,' she decided. 'I'll appeal to him, as the father of my kittens, not to abandon me altogether. Oh, kittens! Poor Fern, poor Moss. Little Sammy, where are you now? How things have changed. And how I wish we were all still together in that pleasant park.'

── 12 ──

A vain appeal

Meanwhile Sammy's progress continued. He was eating better than ever. The girl had noticed Monty's loss of weight and was putting out extra food. She had no desire for the black cat's owners to accuse her of negligence on their return. The problem was, Monty wasn't permitted to partake of the extra meat. Sammy made quite sure of that. And so, as Monty grew leaner, Sammy prospered and grew plumper.

The Church Cat approved of the sleeker, glossier tabby. She taught him daintiness, grace and pride in his appearance. Monty marvelled at the new, foppish Sammy, but he wasn't fooled. Underneath the smooth exterior he knew there was still a tough core.

'Some of the other cats are mocking you,' he told Sammy. 'They laugh at the way you constantly groom your fur, the long periods you spend washing. And I saw one of them mincing along as though copying your walk.'

'Who was that?'

'Spike.'

Sammy stretched. 'Not worth bothering about. They're merely jealous of my refinement.'

The Church Cat enjoyed her power over the tabby. He

would do anything she told him. If Hermione said a certain habit was correct, Sammy adopted it. If she told him something was rough, he avoided it. He practised her drawl, her individual miaow. She was an excellent tutor and was flattered by Sammy's constant attention.

'Do you drink milk?' she asked him.

'Sometimes. When Monty is given it.'

'That's good. You should only drink water when you have to. And always water freshly provided. Anything else is common.'

Sammy thought of some of the muddy puddles he had lapped from in his time and made a grimace.

'Where do you sleep?' the Church Cat asked.

'On the floor.'

'Oh, you should never sleep on the floor. Think of the fleas, the mites, the *dust.* Your fur can't possibly keep its shine if you sleep on the floor.'

'Your coat is magnificent,' Sammy said. 'I could never hope –'

'I know. Of course it's combed regularly. Is yours combed?'

'N-no, 'Sammy answered. 'There's no one to comb mine. I told you. I'm in hiding most of the day. I do all my own grooming.'

'Well, you've certainly made a good start. Keeping clean must be your main object. Don't go out in muddy weather. It really is the *worst* thing for fur.'

Sammy took the Persian's words to heart. He found a chair to lie on and wouldn't stir from the house unless it was quite dry outside. There were plenty of other places to hide in when the girl came. The lack of activity made him plumper still and Monty foresaw the day when his own personal little door wouldn't be wide enough to admit the bulky tabby.

*   *   *

For a couple of days Pinkie kept away from the fox. She guessed the rabbit meat would sustain him for a period, since previously he had survived on the most meagre scraps. She really wanted to rid herself of the taint of the fox and his den before she presented herself at Monty's door.

'I'll have to spruce myself up,' she told herself, 'otherwise Sammy might not even talk to me.' She continued to confine herself to the copse and the riverside, catching a shrew here or a vole there, and once or twice a bird; just enough to keep her going. She didn't see the Pub Cat in all this time.

There was a very wet morning when she huddled under a holly tree in the copse and felt as miserable and lonely as she had ever done in her whole life. She wanted to see Sammy again so badly that, as soon as the wet spell passed, she waited no longer.

'My coat's wet but that's a good thing in a way,' she comforted herself. 'The rain should have washed away those strong smells. Well, I wonder what he'll think of me?'

As she left the tree line and began to cross the field with the gravestones, she saw the Alsatian with its master in the distance. The dog was running free and, with natural exuberance, was cantering along well ahead of the man.

'No use *me* playing dead,' Pinkie muttered. 'I'd never get away with it.' She turned to take refuge amongst the trees.

The dog's eyes picked out her white coat. It was just a blur of movement at such a distance, but the Alsatian at once put on speed to investigate. The dog's acceleration was tremendous and Pinkie dashed under cover and scaled a hawthorn. Her pursuer soon found her and danced about underneath, barking with frustration and making futile leaps to reach her.

Eventually the man came up too, saw the cowering Pinkie in the thorny canopy and swiftly silenced his dog.

'What are you doing so far from home?' the man wondered, mistaking Pinkie for the Pub Cat. 'You look in a bad way. Are you lost?'

Pinkie stared back unblinkingly at what she thought were two enemies, assessing her chances of escape should she have to move. The dog sat quietly now, even thumping its tail as it listened to the friendly tone of its master's voice.

'Perhaps I should try to take you back home,' the man continued. 'Fred' – he turned to his dog – 'you've frightened the poor thing half out of its wits.' He reached both arms upwards, straining to grasp Pinkie, who backed nervously. 'Come on, Snowy,' cooed the man, 'let's get the white cat back to the White Cat.' He leant forward and almost managed to grab Pinkie, who jumped to the ground and shot away with the dog in eager pursuit.

'Fred! *Fred!* Here!' bellowed the Alsatian's owner, but he wasn't quite quick enough. Fred had bowled Pinkie over and into a patch of mud and was just about to seize her. The bedraggled Pinkie took advantage of the dog's hesitation, scrambled to her feet and pelted away back to the field in a blind panic.

'Fred! Come here! Bad boy!' the man shouted. The dog pattered back obediently, looking as though butter wouldn't melt in its mouth. 'All right,' said its owner. 'No harm done, thank goodness. At least the poor cat's going in the right direction.'

Pinkie didn't stop running until she had put the field behind her and could get on top of the high wall behind the row of houses. She was badly scared and, more than ever, yearned for her mate's protection and sympathy.

She forgot all about her appearance. All she wanted to do was to get to Sammy as quickly as possible.

Monty saw her first. Sammy wasn't in the garden and, in fact, was at that moment with the Church Cat. She was showing him off as a sort of exhibit of her tuition in taste and decorum to some of the other cats.

'You're a stranger in our midst,' Monty said to Pinkie. 'My, you're in a state, too. Where have you been and how did you get like that?'

Pinkie didn't want to bandy words with any pet. 'What does it matter to you?' she replied sharply. 'I was attacked by a dog, if that's of any interest. Where's Sammy?'

Monty could guess the tabby was in the vicarage garden but chose not to say so. 'He doesn't stay here *all* the time,' he told Pinkie coyly, 'though he's become much more of a stick-in-the-mud recently. But are *you* all right? Would you like to rest here for a while?'

'No – er – thank you,' the bespattered white cat answered. 'I must see Sammy. It's important. For both of us. I'll go and look for him.'

Monty foresaw trouble. 'Don't go just yet,' he urged. 'He may come back soon. Wait a bit; save yourself a search.'

Pinkie recalled the fright the young human had given her in this very garden. 'No. I can't wait here,' she said. 'I – I must go on. I'll walk along the wall a bit. Maybe I'll see him.'

Monty said no more. He was powerless to influence events and the affairs of Sammy's mate were of no great consequence to him. He watched her go and then, feeling some curiosity after all, climbed the dividing fence to view the outcome.

Sammy was not in the vicarage garden. He and the Church Cat were next door, demonstrating to Spike and

Ling how much Sammy had progressed. Sammy gave the Burmese and the ginger an example of his newly developed drawl, much to their amusement. He had achieved his aim of becoming indistinguishable from the most pampered pet and now he feared nothing. Domino, the black-and-white cat, was hunched behind a clump of daffodils observing the ridiculous spectacle. He nursed plans for revenge on the new Sammy who he felt must have duped him before.

Pinkie reached the spot and looked down unbelievingly. She recognized the haughty Persian and Sammy's slavish copying of her. She was angry and jealous.

'Sammy!' she called sharply and dropped down into the garden.

Sammy turned, saw the muddy cat coming towards him, and didn't immediately realize it was Pinkie.

'Sammy, I need you,' Pinkie pleaded desperately. She ran up, intending to nuzzle him, but Sammy hastily stepped aside.

'Who is this?' demanded the Church Cat, very much on her dignity.

Sammy didn't reply at once, he was so aghast at Pinkie's filthy appearance.

'I'm his mate, if you must know,' Pinkie hissed at Hermione.

'His . . . mate!' the Church Cat breathed, scarcely able to form the words. 'Is this true?' she appealed to Sammy.

'She was,' he muttered savagely, 'but not any longer. No cat with such disregard for cleanliness and – and – elementary hygiene – as *this*' – he spat the word – 'could ever call herself a mate of mine.' He was furious at being humiliated by Pinkie in this way in front of his mentor. He suddenly remembered his audience. 'What are you two gawping at?' he snarled at Ling and Spike, who made haste to leave. 'Don't come near me, soiling me with your grime,' he warned Pinkie. 'What sort of rubbish dump have *you* been living in to present yourself like this?'

'A huge dog tossed me in the mud,' she whimpered. 'I was lucky to get away. I came straight here to find you. Sammy, I – I'm lonely and I'm scared.'

Sammy swallowed hard. 'Look,' he said. 'It's a bit late for that kind of talk now. You wouldn't adopt my plan. You've done nothing to help yourself and now I can't help you either. I've learnt how to behave like a pet again and I don't mean to go back on it. It's my only chance if I don't want to be rounded up. You must take your chance too. You made your choice before and it's no good complaining about it now.'

'But – but – there are rabbits,' Pinkie stammered, 'and I can't catch them by myself. I need help if I'm not to starve.'

'Well, don't look for it here,' the Church Cat told her sourly. 'We don't mix with your kind.'

Sammy remembered this phrase. It wasn't so long since it had been directed at him. How he had come on in the last few days!

Pinkie crept towards Hermione, her tail swishing ominously. 'I wasn't talking to you,' she growled, 'you stuck-up, obese ball of fluff! You don't know Sammy as well as I do. You might think you do, but I could tell you plenty. He may look more like a pet than a real one does, but he's still a savage at heart. Sammy' – she beseeched him one last time – 'don't reject me. Don't sever yourself from me completely. You've forgotten the original point of it all – our escape, our . . . our . . . kittens.'

'Don't come any closer,' Sammy muttered. 'You'll soil my fur. And, anyway, pets don't eat rabbits.' He turned his back on the dishevelled Pinkie. Her last resort – the mention of their kittens – had fallen on deaf ears. He moved away, with Hermione at his side. They looked like clockwork toys, they moved so exactly together.

Pinkie was heartbroken and desolate. She slunk away in a kind of fog of misery, not knowing what to do next. It would have been better to have tried things Sammy's way, however hard that had seemed. What was left for her now? The thought of the decrepit fox as her only companion underlined the isolation of her position. She couldn't bear to return to the cheerlessness of the river bank.

Domino had watched and listened with interest. To him it seemed that Sammy had become flabby and ineffectual. The Church Cat had put her spell on him. It would soon be time to oust the tabby from monopolizing Monty's meat-bowl.

— 13 —

A savage at heart

Sammy's vanity knew no bounds. Horrified as she was, Pinkie marvelled at his transformation. He no longer looked very much like her mate and now he even sounded different. She realized her only hope was to play some trick on him; to show him up for the sham he was in front of his snooty companion. If Sammy were to be rejected by the snobby Persian, he might come to his senses. But how to do it? Well, Pinkie thought grimly, she certainly had plenty of time to herself to devote to the problem.

She recalled Sammy's comments. His words had stung. They had been cruel. She *was* very dirty, though, and she wondered how she was going to clean herself. She jumped from the high wall into some long grass which was soaked by the drizzle. By walking through it she wiped some of the mud from her fur.

She stayed half hidden in the grass. There were several people around on the towpath, but they posed no problem for Snowy, who was more than familiar with large groups of noisy humans. He came stepping purposefully along the edge of the path, his tail hoisted as a permanent flag of greeting to anyone who might show interest in him. He spied Pinkie and joined her.

'I wasn't sure if it was you,' he fibbed. 'You look more like a brown cat than a white one today.'

Pinkie gave him a sullen glance. She wasn't going to explain her appearance for a third time. 'If I lived as you do I could pass for a pub cat,' she told him.

'Oh? Do you have ambitions that way, then?' Snowy asked guardedly.

'Of course not. I told you before, I don't like to be near humans.'

'You get used to them, 'he grunted. 'This – er – mud is a sort of camouflage, is it?'

'Very funny,' Pinkie growled. Snowy smelt of cat food and Pinkie was reminded that she hadn't eaten very much for some time. She could understand how the fox had felt when he had smelt Monty's food on her breath. She didn't want to be bothered by the Pub Cat just now, but he seemed to be enjoying her company.

'Have you seen the tatty old fox again?' he asked.

'Yes.'

'Good. Because I've worked out a way to get at those tormenting lop-ears.'

'Not bunnies again,' Pinkie sighed. 'Why don't you forget them? *You* don't need them.'

'I can't forget them,' Snowy answered fiercely. 'They're always there, tantalizing me, out of reach and getting fatter and fatter . . . Oh, if only the fox were here now, we could get it over with.'

Pinkie had an idea. 'Look, if you're set on eating rabbit, I've a much better plan. Come with me and we'll catch rabbits a-plenty.'

'Wild ones, is it? No, they're scrawny by comparison. You and me and the fox can all profit by those lop-ears. You see, it needs an animal who can dig underneath the cage. Only the old fox could do that.'

Pinkie yawned. Snowy's obsession bored her. 'He

wouldn't come,' she said categorically. 'So I shouldn't get yourself in a lather about it.'

'I can think of a way that would persuade him to come,' the Pub Cat said.

Pinkie was uninterested. 'Really?' Her thoughts were still too full of Sammy and the Church Cat.

'I'd bribe him,' said Snowy. 'Promise him some of my food. Oh, I bet he's never tasted meat like *that* in all his long-suffering life. He'd do *anything* for it. Only he won't get any until he's done what –'

'Yes, yes. I get the drift,' Pinkie interrupted. 'Go and fetch him then. I'll leave you to it. I'm rather tired.'

'Where did you last see him?'

'In his den.'

'Where's that?'

Pinkie explained. 'I can't guarantee he'll still be there,' she added.

'No. No, I understand that. I must hurry,' Snowy said. 'I have to go back to be the pub soon, so there's not much time.'

Pinkie heaved a sigh of relief as he vanished. 'They can do what they like, those two,' she murmured as she lay down. 'I must try to think of a way to get Sammy back.'

The mention of kittens had not been lost on Hermione. The existence of Sammy's one-time mate, low-bred though she was, had come as an unpleasant surprise. The Church Cat nagged Sammy until she had all the facts.

'Was that . . . creature part of your old life?' she wanted to know. 'When you roamed about?'

'Yes, my old life,' Sammy answered. 'When I – you know – was rather wild.'

'Then why is she here now?'

Sammy was flummoxed. 'Well, she . . . she followed me,' he replied unconvincingly. They had returned to the vicarage.

'Where are the kittens?'

'They were captured,' Sammy told her, glad to be able to give a truthful answer. 'In one of the round-ups. We – I mean *she* – couldn't save them.'

The Church Cat had hoped for more information. She had never been mated, and she had been intrigued by the subject of kittens. 'Poor little things,' she murmured before she could stop herself. 'Where were they taken?'

'I don't know. Where do those horrible patrols take any cat?' Sammy began to tremble slightly. The memory of that horrific sequence of events in the park still had the power to disturb him. 'Let's . . . let's not talk about it,' he whispered. 'It's all in the past. I don't like to think too much . . .'

'I understand. But your mate. Your *ex*-mate. What a scruff! How could you –'

'She wasn't always like that,' Sammy cut in quickly, on the defensive. 'I don't know what's happened to her. She once was a very . . . pretty cat,' he ended regretfully.

'Was she indeed?' the Church Cat returned, once again on her dignity. She didn't want to listen to compliments, unless of course they were for her.

'Oh, she never had your grace or style or composure,' Sammy continued. 'But when I first came across her, she was sort of *kittenish* herself.'

The Church Cat had heard all she wanted to hear and possibly more. She was ready to go indoors. From the vicarage window sill she turned proudly and said to Sammy, 'So you're still a savage at heart? Well, maybe I've been misled. We shall see.'

Sammy returned to Monty's garden, a mixture of

feelings welling in his heart. He knew the girl would have brought Monty's meat but, strangely, he didn't feel hungry. He heard Monty's miaows raised in protest.

'You've no right. No right at all. Oh, "When the cat's away . . ." There never was an apter phrase. If Sammy was here, he –'

'He what?' It was Domino's voice and his mouth was full. 'He's no more right to this than me. And he *isn't* here, is he?'

'Who's that, then?' Monty cried gleefully as he saw the tabby breast the fence.

Domino looked out from the house but continued to munch. 'That? That's a cat that's turned soft. Softer than you. Soft as a cushion.'

Monty knew better but he said no more. He awaited results excitedly. Sammy walked straight up to the cat-flap, as bold as brass.

'What's this?' he asked.

'What's it look like?' Domino growled.

'Theft,' came the reply. Sammy wasn't using the Church Cat's drawl now.

'Theft, eh? How is it theft when I eat this if it isn't theft when you do?' Domino was looking a little uneasy. He wasn't absolutely sure of his ground, despite his bravado.

'Monty and I have an arrangement,' Sammy replied reasonably. 'And that arrangement is . . .' In a split second a front paw lashed out and Sammy's claws raked across Domino's face.

The black-and-white cat let out a howl of pain. He hadn't been on his guard and was taken completely by surprise. Monty gloated. But Sammy wasn't finished. He leapt on Domino and dug all his claws deep into the other cat's hide. 'Seems you didn't learn your lesson last time,' he snarled. Domino struggled free and offered no retaliation. He couldn't escape quickly enough. Sammy grinned. 'I suppose I am still a savage at heart,' he muttered to himself. 'Pinkie was right. But as long as I don't look like one, I'm safe.' He glanced down. The meat-bowl was all but empty.

When the towpath was quieter Pinkie ventured to the water's edge to see if she could catch a fish. In the river shallows small fry were darting about. She dabbled a paw and tried to hook one out without success. She leant out farther. A larger fish cruised close. In her excitement Pinkie half jumped into the water, soaking herself but missing the fish. A boat chugged downriver, sending its wash rippling towards the bank. Pinkie, intent on her fishing, was almost submerged by the rapid wavelets which broke over her back. She retreated hastily and shook herself. Most of the mud was washed from her fur but she was cold and hungry. At that moment Snowy came tripping along from the direction of the railway bridge. Pinkie skulked in the riverside vegetation, hoping the Pub Cat would miss her. He seemed in a hurry. Some slight movement caught his eye.

'Been swimming?' he quipped. 'You *are* in a state. But you look almost white again.'

'Did you see the fox?' Pinkie muttered resentfully.

'I saw him, yes, in that smelly hole he calls his den. He said he'd come tonight if his legs don't give out first. I knew the promise of meat would entice him. And you' – Snowy looked Pinkie up and down – 'you could use a good feed. You come too. At dusk.'

Pinkie was tempted. 'I might and I might not,' she said.

'You will,' Snowy answered confidently. 'You can't afford not to. You're ravenous. Did you land a fish?'

'How did you . . . ? No,' Pinkie growled.

'Cats don't readily take to water, do they?' the Pub
Cat said knowingly. 'Slippery customers, fish. If you're
reduced to fishing to survive, you'll come tonight.' He
ran on, calling behind him, 'Don't carp at my offer.'

Pinkie was far from amused. She was so uncomfortable she could only think of getting herself dry. The
cloudy sky was broken by patches of blue. Gleams of
fitful sunshine bathed the riverside here and there.
Pinkie, with a cat's unerring instinct, found the warmest
and sunniest place against the high wall. She napped on
and off, drowsing as she gradually dried off.

Unknown to Pinkie, another cat, a stranger to her,
was seeking her. Domino, just like the Church Cat, had
witnessed the scene between Sammy and his mate. After
his latest humiliating brush with the tabby, his lust for
revenge was greater than ever. Sammy had wounded
him in more than one way and he was determined to get
even. He saw Pinkie as the key to his chance of doing it.
She too had suffered. Sammy had scorned and insulted
her and she must be bitter against him. Domino paced
through the gardens, looking everywhere for the little
white cat with the soiled coat. Finally he climbed to the
top of the wall and looked along it. Pinkie, a white blur
against the brickwork, caught his eye. He miaowed to
himself with satisfaction. 'There's my ally,' he hissed.

—14—

After the bunnies

Pinkie awoke to find a plump vole looking for its own food within pouncing distance. No sooner had she seen it than she slew it and began to eat with tremendous gusto.

'That's what your mate's selfishness has brought you to, isn't it?'

Pinkie glanced up without interrupting her feeding. Directly above her on the high wall was Domino the black-and-white cat.

'While he feasts you're famished,' he continued.

'What's it to you?' Pinkie mumbled.

'I thought you might like to even things up a bit.'

'What are you talking about? Why are you so concerned?' Pinkie demanded.

'Because of this!' Domino snapped, bending his head so that Pinkie could see what Sammy's claws had done. There was dried blood on Domino's face.

'Oh, you've been in a fight,' Pinkie purred. 'Did Sammy do that to you?' Despite everything, she still felt a strange pride in the tabby's power. She swallowed the rest of her kill and waited for the other cat's reply.

'Well, I didn't do it myself,' Domino growled. He jumped down and now Pinkie saw other wounds along his back. 'He's gone too far this time,' the black-and-white cat raged. 'This was a peaceful neighbourhood before he swaggered in, upsetting everybody. Monty gives up his food to him. And your mate rewards him by taking over his home. He bullies all the other cats and drives you out so that he can hobnob with that supercilious Persian.'

Pinkie blinked and stared. There was a lot of truth in Domino's words. It was obvious the black-and-white cat wanted rid of Sammy. 'Sammy doesn't belong where he is – you're right,' she said slowly. 'I'd like him back with me, away from human dens and that blue fur-ball. But he's under her influence.'

'He doesn't know how absurd he looks, aping every aspect of her priggish behaviour.' And Domino gave an illustration by mincing along with the Church Cat's dainty steps.

Pinkie didn't know whether to be amused by the sight or annoyed that Sammy had become the butt of the other cat's ridicule. 'What do you propose?' she asked.

'That we get him caught by Monty's provider.'

'The – the human?' Pinkie didn't like the idea but she was curious.

'Yes, the girl. If she discovers him in the house, that would change everything.'

'It certainly would,' Pinkie agreed enthusiastically. 'How would we go about it?'

'Simple. We both get into the house through Monty's little door and then hang around until the next lot of food is brought. If *we're* found there – especially you – the young human will be suspicious and search for other interlopers. Sammy will be driven away, along with us.'

Pinkie naturally recalled how she had been scared away by the girl on a previous occasion. 'No, no, I can't do it,' she stammered. 'It's clever, but I can't be part of it. I won't go into that human's den. I don't trust humans.'

Domino saw she was fearful. 'You've . . . always lived wild, have you?'

'Always.'

'There's nothing to be afraid of. Really. You wouldn't get hurt.'

'No. No, I won't. I can't.' Pinkie was trembling. She started to walk away. 'I – I'm not a pet. I'm not like you.'

'You won't help yourself then,' Domino called after her irritably. 'The Church Cat's beaten you!'

Pinkie ran. She didn't want to hear any more. To deliberately put herself in the path of a human! And one who had scared her before! Never! As for Domino, he knew he had no chance of getting into Monty's house without Pinkie behind him. Sammy would see to that. So he was left to snarl his frustration to himself.

By dusk Pinkie had managed to catch two more mice. Her stomach wasn't grumbling any more but she did hanker after some real meat. It was a warm, still spring evening. Without actually thinking about it, she sauntered along in the direction of the White Cat. She wasn't interested in Snowy's silly scheme for the lop-ears, but his offer of food certainly held an attraction.

Cheerful human voices could be heard coming from the pub. It was warm enough for all the windows and doors to be open for the first time that year. Pinkie sat under the pub sign with the portrait of Snowy and waited for the real Pub Cat to appear. She wasn't going any further on her own.

Darkness fell. Pinkie listened nervously to the voices, which were growing steadily more boisterous. She was on the point of hurrying away when Snowy suddenly called from the side of the building.

'I thought you'd be there. Come on, what are you waiting for?'

'You, of course,' Pinkie replied bluntly. She crept round to join him and saw he was on his own. 'I told you the fox wouldn't come,' she said.

'Well, you're wrong. He's already here, lurking in the garden. He came by a different route. He looks pretty desperate.'

'That makes a change,' Pinkie commented sarcastically, following the Pub Cat through the shadows. 'Have you allowed him to eat?'

'Not yet. I told you, he has to get at the –'

'I know. I know. The precious bunnies.'

'It'll be a cinch. The ground's soft and damp. Even a scarecrow of a fox like him will find digging easy.'

The cats threaded their way through the car park and reached the pub garden. 'I'll stay out of sight,' said Pinkie. 'I won't be of any use here.'

'Of course you will be,' the Pub Cat answered quickly. 'We'll need you to help snare the bunnies. You don't think they'll just stand around while a fox tunnels under their cage? They'll dart into their box immediately. So we have to haul them out of it.'

'Oh no. You never told me any of this,' Pinkie argued. 'The noise will bring some of your nosy humans out. *I* don't want to be involved.'

'What are you here for, then?' Snowy snapped.

'Well, you made me an offer of food. And that's all. No mention of –'

'Earning it?' the Pub Cat interjected angrily.

Pinkie saw the fox lying, panting, in the darkest corner of the garden. He was swallowing constantly, driven half mad by the smell of the lop-ears and the lure of the good cat meat he had been promised. Pinkie was positive something would go wrong and the wretched beast would be disappointed. Once again she felt a wave of sympathy.

'All right,' she said to Snowy. 'I'll do what I can. But only as long as we're not disturbed.'

'*That's* the spirit,' the Pub Cat said eagerly. 'Well, Fox! Let's start.'

The fox slunk on his belly towards the cage. The rabbits froze, then shot into their sleeping quarters. The fox began to scrape at the ground on one side with his front paws. He had no strength and he paused frequently, taking great gulping breaths. Snowy and Pinkie hunched nearby. Snowy's tail twitched constantly with impatience. 'I could do a better job myself,' he complained.

'Why don't you, then?' Pinkie challenged him. 'Is it fair to make the fox struggle like that?'

'He'll be rewarded eventually,' the Pub Cat replied.

'You should have rewarded him first,' Pinkie countered. 'The meat would have given him the energy to dig properly.'

The fox battled on. His breathing became more and more strained. In the end it was Pinkie, not Snowy, who went to assist. She edged forward and saw that the fox had made a shallow scrape under the wire of the rabbits' run.

'Rest yourself,' she advised him. 'I'm the smallest of us. I can probably get myself under there.' She tugged away at some loose earth and, flattening her body, squeezed underneath the wire. The fox sank to the ground, utterly spent.

'Catch them, Pinkie!' the Pub Cat shrilled.

The panic-stricken lop-ears scratched and scrabbled at their box, trying in vain to get out. The fox couldn't bear the suspense any more. He lifted up his head and yapped sharply. This was the worst thing he could have done.

The wild creature's bark was picked up instantly inside the pub by a large dog who was lying by its owner's seat, head on paws. It was the very Alsatian that had chased Pinkie in the copse. Now it jumped up in excitement and, before it could be prevented, dashed out of the open pub door, its hackles raised, and rushed towards the unsuspecting animals. Pinkie was trapped inside the rabbit run, the fox too exhausted to flee. Only Snowy was able to move. The Alsatian was almost on them by the time the Pub Cat started to run. Instinctively the dog chased him, ignoring the fox playing dead. It caught him in two bounds and seized him in its jaws, crushing him terribly. The fox somehow hauled himself to the safety of a hiding place. In any case the dog was too busy shaking its prize around, growling ferociously, to notice him. The terrified Pinkie tried to get inside the rabbits' box, although in effect protected by the cage. At this point the dog's owner, who had thought the previous encounter with a white cat had also been with Snowy, came running and shouting to his dog to let go. Other people clustered around.

'Oh, Fred,' the man moaned, 'you horrible dog! You've really done for him this time!'

The Alsatian dropped the lifeless cat, who was bleeding from several deep gashes. It knew it had done wrong and now it cowered, its tail drooping between its legs and with ears laid back, obviously expecting a blow. There were horrified gasps and cries from the onlookers who knew the Pub Cat well. Accusations were raised against the careless owner of the Alsatian. Finally the landlord was fetched. The small crowd fell back as

Snowy's master picked up the cat's body and cradled it tenderly. The man turned sad eyes on Fred's owner.

'Why did you let this happen?' he whispered. 'My cat was harmless. He was a bit wild when I found him but I gave him a good home and he responded to it. We were friends.' He was quite overcome.

The other man, shamefaced, babbled hopeless apologies. People raised their voices again, saying such a fierce dog should never be allowed off the lead.

'Is it . . . is it too late to call the vet?' Fred's owner stammered.

'Look at him,' the landlord answered, showing the limp white body in his arms. 'Your dog nearly tore him in two. Don't you ever bring it into my pub again.' He turned his back and stepped sorrowfully back indoors. A hush descended on the crowd. The Alsatian was led away, yanked fiercely on a chokingly shortened chain, by a downcast owner. No one had noticed Pinkie.

Then, abruptly, a woman started to gesticulate, calling out wonderingly, 'Look. Look at that, everyone. Another white cat. There, in that cage! How extraordinary. Whatever is it doing there? It looks like Snowy's double!'

— 15 —

Stuck

A knot of people began to advance on the rabbits' hutch. Pinkie was more frightened than ever. She ducked under the wire at the scrape but, in her desperation to escape, didn't use sufficient care. The wire caught on her back and she let out a howl. A woman hastened to free her, which only made Pinkie wrench harder. She was almost clear when the woman swooped, gathering her up into her arms. Pinkie struggled but was held firmly.

'Oh look, poor thing. It's torn its back badly,' the woman said. Pinkie was indeed bleeding freely.

'What a strange business,' a man said. 'First Snowy and then another white cat injured. Who does this one belong to? And what's been going on?'

No one was able to provide the answer. The woman who had rescued Pinkie said, 'I don't think this one belongs to anybody. It looks like a stray to me. It certainly hasn't been cared for. I'll take it indoors. It needs some attention.'

The fox continued to lie low until all the people had returned to the pub lounge. Then the battered creature had a most unexpected piece of luck. With Pinkie removed from their cage the lop-ears had calmed down and now one of them discovered the gap underneath the wire for itself. It wriggled through and, all alarms forgotten, began to hop confidently about the garden. The other rabbit wasn't slow to follow. The fox didn't stir but his old eyes were almost popping out of his head. The rabbits knew nothing about his presence in the shadows and moved around without caution. Eventually one of them skipped too close to the drooling fox. The ancient hunter just had enough strength and technique remaining to him to grab this chance. He fell on the rabbit and with his few surviving teeth scored his first major kill for ages. The other rabbit, of course, bolted, but the fox wasn't bothered. He half carried, half dragged his prey away to a more secluded spot where he wasted no time in devouring it down to the bone. 'What a turn-up,' he chuckled to himself. 'Everything comes to those who wait.' And, with the other rabbit loose, he had some hopes of coming across that, too, before long.

The landlord of The White Cat was too upset about Snowy just then to take much heed of Pinkie. But he allowed the woman who had rescued her to put her in Snowy's cat basket after his wife had bathed Pinkie's wounds a little. No one in the pub had any idea to whom the strange white cat belonged, nor where she had come from. People came to the conclusion that she had been abandoned or that she was a stray. The upshot was that the landlord's wife put a call through to the local animal home, who said they would send an officer to collect the invalid. Pinkie was shut in a room on her own to await her fate.

She had been frantic at first at the turn of events. Gradually, though, the obvious concern and kindness of her rescuer, who had a wonderfully soothing voice, helped to quieten her down. Her ordeal had tired her out and that and the warmth of the room eventually sent her to sleep. The landlord's wife put some milk and pet food down near Pinkie's basket. Doing this comforted her a little for the loss of her own cat. She and her husband had to keep Pinkie safe for the night since she wouldn't be picked up until the morning. Then, initially, she would be cared for in the animal home. So it seemed that Pinkie's separation from Sammy was to become permanent.

The tabby continued to rule the roost in Monty's sitting-room and garden. Domino didn't enter this territory again, to say nothing of Ling or Spike. Only the Church Cat dared to do so, but by now Sammy was so content with his pet-like appearance and behaviour that he didn't have much need of her. He still admired Hermione enormously and when she was around no thought of Pinkie ever entered his head. But at other times he fell to wondering about his one-time mate, even hoping that she would perhaps come to look for him. Provided, of course, that she had cleaned herself up first.

Monty the black cat was becoming increasingly fed up. Despite the fact that Sammy had kept his promise and deterred other cats from stealing Monty's food, the tabby had grown greedier and more dominating with every day that passed. Monty yearned for his owners to return and set him free from this peculiar sort of bondage. The girl never seemed to suspect anything unusual was going on. She never saw Sammy indoors or outdoors, but continued to increase the amount of food provided because of Sammy's appetite, as though Monty had somehow doubled himself.

Sammy preened, ate, purred satisfaction, slept and groomed himself again. He didn't appear to give any thought to the fact that his occupation of Monty's home was temporary and that one day there would be a rude awakening for him. In the end Monty couldn't bear it any longer and brought the subject up himself.

'What will you do when the master and mistress come back?'

Sammy yawned widely. He had just eaten his fill and he felt content and sleepy. 'Oh well,' he said, 'I'll face that when it happens. No point in thinking about it at the moment, is there?'

'I wish you would think about it,' Monty replied. 'This arrangement will have to come to an end soon. And then where will you go?'

'Perhaps I'll take up residence with Domino,' Sammy answered flippantly. 'What does it matter to you, anyway?'

Monty glowered but said no more. He couldn't himself shift Sammy and could only grit his teeth.

And then one day something happened which did change the state of affairs. Sammy was lying in the garden for once. Monty was roaming elsewhere. The constant presence of the tabby was so irksome to the black cat that he would leave his home area for a while just to get away from Sammy. Sammy had eaten particularly well that morning. In fact he had demolished the entire contents of Monty's bowl. Monty hadn't felt hungry. He was slightly off-colour and Sammy had made the most of it. Now he was sleeping it off.

A sudden shower of rain woke him up and he trotted to the cat-flap. He put his head through and his front legs and then, with his body half in and half out of the little door, he stuck fast. Sammy had finally grown so fat that the cat-flap was too narrow for him. The tabby strained and heaved but hardly managed to move a jot. Indeed he seemed to become even

more firmly wedged. The rain brought Monty running for shelter too. He soon found Sammy barring
his way.

'Hurry up,' he urged the tabby. 'I'm getting wet
here.'

'I . . . can't,' Sammy gasped. 'I'm stuck. I can't move.'

'Oh, so this is what you've brought yourself to,' Monty
said angrily. 'The way you've eaten and eaten . . . enough
for two cats. Well, you can't stay there. You'll have to
back out. You're stopping me from entering my own
home.'

'I know, I know. I'm sorry.' Sammy had the grace to
apologize. 'But I can't go forwards *or* backwards!'

Monty was livid. This greedy animal who had battened
on him and scoffed his food was now denying him
shelter too. 'The girl will find you here,' he reminded
Sammy. 'What then?'

'*Oh!*' the tabby wailed, wriggling hopelessly. 'Monty,
please give me a push or a nudge or something. This
hurts.'

'It serves you right,' said Monty, who had suddenly
become much more courageous now that Sammy was
at a disadvantage. 'But no, I won't push. You must try
to back out. Otherwise you'll be indoors for good.'

Sammy understood the reasoning but he simply
couldn't reverse, try as he might. At last Monty, who
was getting wetter and wetter, decided it was better
Sammy should be trapped in the house rather than
in his cat-flap. With some malice he lowered his head
and butted Sammy hard in the rear. Sammy howled but
his body was jolted forward. He heaved and tugged once
more and at last freed himself with a jerk, like a cork
coming out of a bottle.

Monty leapt after him. 'This is a fine affair,' the
black cat complained as he watched Sammy trying

to lick his aching sides. 'You'll be discovered now for sure.'

'Maybe not,' Sammy answered, though he didn't feel very confident. 'I can still hide, can't I?'

'There are some things you can't hide,' Monty retorted. 'And if you can't get into the garden . . .'

Sammy understood. Monty had no cat litter. He looked glumly at the black cat.

'What can't be buried will be found,' Monty said unnecessarily.

'That's true,' Sammy admitted. Then he suddenly gave Monty a large grin. 'But the girl would be bound to suspect you. She knows nothing about me and so it'll be you who'll be punished!'

Monty blinked. He hadn't thought of that. Then he became very angry. Suddenly he wasn't scared of Sammy any more. 'You mean you . . . you would actually let me take the blame? Let me suffer . . . after all you've had from me?' he shrilled.

'I wouldn't choose to, but it's unavoidable, isn't it?' Sammy replied airily. 'If I reveal myself to the young human, I'll be booted out at once. Why should I risk that?'

Monty was speechless.

'But really,' Sammy went on, 'I don't want you to get into trouble. I can hold on. And I won't eat any more today *or* tomorrow. Then maybe I'll be able to get through your door again.'

Monty calmed down. 'I hope you're right,' he muttered. 'And now you'd better find somewhere to hide. Upstairs.'

'Show me,' Sammy said. He'd never been upstairs before.

Monty led him to the stairs. 'Follow me,' he called behind him. They ran up and Monty went into a small bedroom at the end of the landing. 'Stay in here,' he told Sammy. 'The girl won't know you're around. For a while, anyway,' he added. 'If she comes anywhere near, you can get out of sight under the bed.'

'All right,' Sammy grunted. 'But when she's gone I shan't hang around. I'll come down and join you. There's no water up here, is there?'

'Of course not. There's only the bowl in the kitchen.' Monty thought for a few moments. 'You can come down for a drink, but you'll have to return here afterwards. In case of accidents,' he stressed.

'Very well,' said Sammy.

When the girl arrived in the evening Sammy was well out of sight and listening carefully. She wasn't in the house long. Monty looked gloomily at the pile of meat in his bowl. He had very little appetite. He ate a small amount, then went to his bed. During the night Sammy came for some water. Monty was sleeping. Luckily Sammy wasn't feeling hungry, since he had been so greedy earlier, so he was able to ignore the food-bowl.

Next morning the girl was surprised to find some meat remaining – in fact the greater portion of the recent meal. This hadn't happened before. She wondered if Monty was quite well, but decided he looked healthy enough, and so left the meat as it was, without adding to it. By the evening of that day the meat was dried up and stale. Monty had eaten no more and Sammy was fighting his stomach's demands to be filled. The girl now realized something was wrong. She telephoned Monty's owners at their holiday address and explained the situation. They asked her if she could get Monty to Donald Fairhurst, the local vet, to be examined. The girl agreed and arranged to telephone again with his verdict.

During that night Sammy's hunger could no longer
be denied. Stale food or not, he had to have it. He
had become so used to eating regularly that the food
languishing in Monty's bowl became more important
to him than the difficulty of getting through Monty's
door. He began to eat and Monty made no attempt to
stop him. Immediately after he had cleared the bowl,
Sammy remembered the cat-flap.

'Well, I haven't eaten *that* much,' he muttered to
himself with some feeling of guilt. 'I'd better try to get
out anyway.' He pushed his head through the cat flap
and slowly, very slowly, eased his body through. Just as
before, at the halfway point he stuck. His sides were still
sore from his last effort and it was too painful for him
to wriggle or squeeze. He tried backing, with the same
result. 'Oh, why did I do this?' he wailed. 'I didn't have
to try *now*. I was better off indoors. Monty! Help me!'

Monty was in no position to help. He was feeling very
unwell and lay listlessly on his bed. He had no intention
of going to Sammy's rescue this time.

'Monty! *Monty!* Please!' Sammy pleaded frantically.
'I'm stuck fast and I'm in real trouble!'

Monty recalled Sammy's attitude about *his* getting
into trouble and answered feebly, 'You deserve to be.
Your greed has caught up with you. The girl will release
you in the morning.'

Sammy was aghast. He couldn't allow that to happen.
It would mean a return to scavenging, living in the
open and all that that would entail. He thought of
Pinkie and her disreputable appearance. How long
would his beautiful clean coat and pet's manners last
if he were forced to join her again? 'I must bear the
pain,' he told himself. 'I've got to get free.' He braced
his front legs and strained. A long agonized miaow
pierced the darkness. '*Ooouw!*' His body hardly moved

a fraction. Sammy let his head drop. 'No, it's no good,' he moaned. The narrow opening held him like a vice. And that was where the girl found him in the morning.

— 16 —

Freed

The girl didn't notice Sammy straight away. Her first concern was for Monty, who hadn't moved from his bed in the kitchen.

'Poor Monty,' the girl said, stroking him compassionately. 'You don't look right at all. I must phone the vet now and see if he can have a look at you today, even though it's Sunday.'

Luckily the vet was a family friend and agreed to her request. Monty didn't even raise his head. But in the sitting-room Sammy tensed, a prisoner waiting for his punishment. The girl was about to leave the house, with Monty in his basket, when she suddenly remembered the food-bowl. She thought she had better clear it up then in case the vet kept Monty at the surgery for a while. She set the basket down in the hall and went to the sitting-room, where she saw Sammy's hindquarters and tail protruding from the cat flap.

'What's this? Shoo!' she cried, clapping her hands. Sammy, trembling like a leaf, didn't budge. 'Shoo, I say! Off you go!' the girl shouted. Then she spied the food-bowl. 'Oh, so that's it. Stealing food!' She marched up to the tabby and gave his rear end the most gentle of nudges with her foot. Sammy hardly moved, but he howled. Now the girl understood the problem.

'You're caught in there, are you? Well, that's a just reward for thieving. I don't recognize you at all. Whose pet are you, I wonder?' She bent down and tried to push Sammy on his way. 'Plump chap, aren't you?' she commented. Then the girl put a hand either side of the tabby's body and pushed gently inwards. It gave Sammy just that tiny bit more room for manoeuvre and it made all the difference. He heaved himself clear with another howl of pain and raced off down the garden.

The girl watched him go and suddenly an idea struck her. Was this animal the reason for Monty's illness? Had it been visiting regularly and robbing the black cat of his food? Was poor weak Monty half starved? She hurried back to the hall, snatched up the cat basket and rushed off to her appointment at the vet's, worried to death that she had been negligent of her charge.

Sammy, stiff and sore, but relieved to have escaped from his prison, was at a loss to know where to go next. He thought again of Pinkie and then he thought of Hermione. And, because he didn't know where Pinkie was, but he did know where to find the Church Cat, he set off for the vicarage.

The Persian was basking on a warm flagstone in the garden. She rolled over playfully when she saw Sammy, but the tabby was in no mood for games. All that he had gained, all that he had learnt from the Church Cat's manners and behaviour, was in jeopardy.

'My, you *have* been eating well,' she drawled admiringly. 'You look so stout and – and smooth.'

'Yes,' Sammy agreed. 'I feel I am.' He fell at once into the Persian's mode of speech. 'But I fear the good times are over for me. My arrangement with Monty has –' He stopped suddenly and listened hard. Was he mistaken? Tramp, tramp . . . Surely not? Yes . . . Tramp! Tramp! Tramp!

The Church Cat, unperturbed by the distant sound, watched in amazement as Sammy reacted. All sense seemed to have left him. He dashed one way and then back again, then off in another, without any sense of purpose. He was in a panic.

'What is it? What's wrong?' the Persian called.

'Can't you hear it?' Sammy cried. 'It's . . . oh, it's . . . the patrols! They're here again!' He wasn't speaking in her tones now. He was in a sort of frenzy. But, seeing the Church Cat's complete lack of concern, he was puzzled enough to stop still for a moment. To the tramping feet was now added a roll of drums, and then music began to blare.

'Patrols?' Hermione repeated. 'What patrols? What do you mean, Sammy?'

'Oh, how can you possibly understand?' he gasped. 'You – the supreme pet; so safe, so assured. How could such a thing concern you?' He was quaking, glancing around for somewhere safe to bury himself. And then, in the midst of his fear, came a sudden anguished thought. Pinkie! Where was she? Was she safe? All at once he was back with the little white cat, his mate, in the park, running, running . . . 'I must find her! Warn her!' he cried to the mystified Persian. And the Church Cat was forgotten in the urgency of the moment.

Sammy smothered his fear and thought hard. The riverside! That must be his best bet. Pinkie was likely to be somewhere near the water. Yet he hadn't seen her for quite a time . . . Oh, why had he turned his back on her so completely? She was alone and defenceless. Already the veneer of pet behaviour that Sammy had assumed was peeling away. He left the Church Cat without another word and made for the high wall. The noise of the scout troop's band and the marching feet thumped against his sensitive ears. Sammy tried desperately to blot it out.

He soon reached the riverside, where the noise wasn't quite so penetrating. He began his search. First he went towards the pub. Of course he found no trace of her. Pinkie had been whisked away from that place. Then Sammy retraced his steps, calling regularly, and pressed on towards the bridge. When he saw no sign of her in that direction either he began to dread the worst. He reached the bridge and looked around nervously. This was new territory for Sammy. He called once or twice in a fairly hopeless way. Then he noticed a hole in the bank, and stepped up to it. A faint scuffling sound came briefly from inside. Sammy's hopes were raised. Could it be? He thought he detected Pinkie's scent, but there was a much stronger odour dominating.

'Pinkie? Are you there?'

The old fox was in his den, trying to get comfortable. He limped to the opening and saw the tabby cat, who drew back in dismay.

'Who are you?' the dishevelled beast grunted.

'I'm Sammy. I mean – I'm looking for my mate. I didn't realize – I'm sorry to disturb you.'

'Mate?'

'Yes – a little white cat. You wouldn't know, I suppose, anything . . . about her?' Sammy asked haltingly.

'Oh yes. I know her. Well, I *did* know her. We tried to catch rabbits together. With the other cat.'

'The – other cat?'

'Yes. The one who got killed by the dog. Ugh! It was messy.'

Sammy's stomach lurched. 'But . . . the little white cat . . . she's still alive?'

'The female? She was when I last saw her. But then she was taken away.'

'No! The patrols?' gasped Sammy, barely able to speak.

'Patrols? What's that?'

'The . . . the humans who come –'

'Oh, humans, yes,' said the fox. '*They* took her all right. I was hiding. And then I got one of those fat rabbits. Ah, what a feast!' The fox swallowed hard, closing his eyes at the delightful memory. 'I'm still hopeful of finding the other one.'

Sammy wasn't listening to him any more. Only the news he had dreaded had reached his ears. Pinkie taken! Then it was all up with her. And he had turned his back. Oh, why hadn't she listened to him? Done as he had done? Looked after herself, made herself change . . . Now what was he to do? His pet days were over. There was nothing left for him here except loneliness and hardship . . . How lonely and hard Pinkie must have found the days! He had been entirely selfish. And now he would experience what she had. On his own, like her. Unless . . .

The fox still rambled on about rabbits and other things of no interest to Sammy, who turned from him and began to walk away. The noise of marching feet, the blare of bugles, had ceased. Was it too late? Too late for Sammy to be captured? That was all he wished now. To be taken where Pinkie had gone . . . to join her, perhaps for the last time . . .

'Thank you, Fox,' he muttered without glancing back. 'I'm grateful to you. At least I know.'

The fox's voice petered out and he watched the tabby propel himself into a sprint. He regretted the cat's departure. He had been without any kind of company himself since the events in the pub garden. 'Cats!' he croaked. 'They come and they go . . .'

Sammy steeled himself to go into harm's way. He

could hear human voices, many voices, and they were all around the church. He believed he was courting capture by the patrols. And that was what he wanted. It was *all* he wanted. But he had one last fear. It was that he would be ignored; overlooked as a well-kept, well-fed pet. What Sammy had aimed for all along could now cheat him out of finding Pinkie again.

By way of the churchyard he came across a throng of people in front of the church. Some, the younger ones, were in uniform. Sammy thought he recognized that uniform. It was a dark colour like the dark overalls of the men who had rounded up his kittens in the park. With a wildly beating heart, but thinking only of Pinkie, he got in amongst them. The boys didn't pay him much attention. One or two bent down to give him a half-hearted stroke. Others warned their friends not to tread on his feet. Sammy mingled with them, trying to be noticed, to be snatched . . .

It was hopeless. He was too clean, too plump. He had the look of a cosseted pet. He was no more likely to be seized than the Church Cat. He should have rolled in some dirt, fallen in a puddle, anything that would have made him a target. Now the people were entering the church. Sammy sat against a wall. Soon he was alone. The van, he decided, must have already left, the van with Pinkie inside it . . .

'I shall never see her again,' he said to himself. 'My vagabond mate.' He remembered how he had crossed London to rejoin her after they had been separated once before. Then he had used his wits and, with help from other creatures, had found his way, bit by bit, back to her side. He jumped up. 'And I can do it again!' he mewed to the empty street. 'I'll go back to the fox. He must know more. He can guide me, perhaps. Don't forget me, Pinkie. I'm not finished yet!'

— 17 —

Human care

Pinkie had certainly not forgotten Sammy. She had been languishing in a pen in the animal home for some days, loathing every moment of her captivity. Around her other animals paced their cages, ate or slept just as she did. She still couldn't fully grasp what had happened; it had all been so sudden and unexpected. Yet here she was, accepting food and treatment from those human hands she had distrusted all her life. Friendly words, soothing caresses – she was becoming used to all of it. She wondered about Sammy and what would happen to him. She knew his new life could be only temporary. He had been foolish and unkind, but she knew his plan to act the pet had blinded him to all other considerations, including his mate.

Pinkie also thought about Snowy and his horrible end. The Alsatian had made her scared of all dogs. She knew there were dogs not far from her cage now. She heard them and smelt them. And, because she had no idea what was to become of her, she was afraid that she might not always be protected from them. This was a constant fear. However, there were many cats, too, some of whom she could talk to. They soon knew all there was to know about each other, and they talked endlessly of their fate. Some thought of escape, others said it was impossible. There were rumours that there was another place that, eventually, all of them would be taken to. But no one knew what or where that was. They only knew that sometimes one of them was taken away by a small group of humans, sometimes by an individual, but all with faces none of them had ever seen before.

Pinkie trusted the people who fed her and cared for her. She ate well and put on weight. Her wounds healed quickly. But her one desire was to be set free to take up again the only life she really understood – with Sammy or without him. Like the other animals she wondered if one day she would be taken away by strange humans to some other place. She had been brought to the home by strangers; not rounded up in the open by the frightening patrols, but gently and carefully carried from the pub, from *indoors*, by a different kind of people. It was all very confusing and puzzling for a cat who had never been used to humans of any sort and preferred to avoid them.

Her old life with Sammy and the kittens in the London park seemed distant indeed. So much had happened since they had been rescued by Buster and hidden in his owner's car. And now she waited helplessly as the humans decided her future.

Meanwhile Sammy was hoping to get on her trail. He set off for the fox's lair in better spirits. His new quest excited but at the same time daunted him. Already the period spent in Monty's home was beginning to seem like a kind of dream. Sammy had returned to his old way of life now. And, although it had been forced on him, he was oddly content. Once again he had to depend on himself alone and, rather vainly, he thought that that was when he was at his best.

The fox was fast asleep and took some waking. 'Oh,

it's you again,' he mumbled once he had been brought round. 'I'm still tired. My den's so uncomfortable it takes me an age to get settled. I don't seem to have slept at all. I suppose you want to know where the rabbits are?'

'Rabbits?' Sammy echoed. 'No, no, that's not why I'm here.'

The fox said, 'Isn't it? That's what the white cat was after. And she did manage to catch one. She even left me some of the meat. Have you left anything for me? I need all the help I can get. And that's very little usually.'

Sammy was exasperated. He wanted vital information about Pinkie and this ancient creature was chattering on endlessly about other things. 'Listen, please,' he interrupted. 'Please, Fox. I need *your* help. You saw the little white cat taken. Where did it happen? And did you see which way the humans went?'

'It happened at the pub. Where the rabbits were kept. She got injured and the humans took her inside. That was the last I saw of her.'

'The pub! Where's that?'

'By the river. Where all the humans gather to make noise.'

'You mean the place by the high wall? Oh, yes. I know it. I should do!' Sammy recalled that it was the very spot where he and Pinkie had fled from the car. 'You say she was injured?' he prompted.

'She got caught up in some wire. One of the humans rescued her. She wanted to look after her. You know how they are about your sort. Me, I've never been given any kind of consideration by them. I've been hurt, wounded, chased, but never looked after. I did know a fox once who had been hit by a car and was taken to some place by humans who cared for him until he recovered. Then they let him go. But never me. Still, I don't complain. I prefer to –'

'So it wasn't a round-up!' Sammy cried exultantly. 'Oh, I've got to find her. She was my mate, you see. I don't understand all this talk about rabbits. But if I see one, I'll try to catch it for you. You've put me on the right track and I'm grateful.'

'You'll be back, then?' the old fox asked eagerly.

'Well, yes, probably.' Sammy didn't want to commit himself. 'I can't promise you that rabbit, but I'll do what I can.'

All thought of rabbits instantly left Sammy's head as he trotted along. He could think only of Pinkie, safe in some kind human's care. He knew all about the kindlier side of humans, having been born the son of a pet cat himself. He didn't think it would be difficult to find his mate. If people could go in and out of a pub, so could a cat!

'How lucky,' he said to himself light-heartedly, 'that the patrol ignored me earlier. *I* could have been captured while Pinkie was safe all the time.' Sammy still believed the dark-shirted scouts were a round-up team. 'Well, I proved my theory. If you look like a pet, they don't want to bother with you.'

But he had to accept that he was now effectively a stray again. Very soon he would have to resume providing food for himself. Then, gradually, the rough life would erase his smart new appearance and he would be vulnerable once more. At present, though, nothing could dampen his optimism. He was buoyed up by the unexpected good news and he reached the pub garden full of confidence.

The noise and bustle of the pub that Sunday lunchtime held no alarms for Sammy. He wasn't afraid of humans of the ordinary, boisterous kind. He knew

Pinkie was unlikely to be found outside the building, so that meant he'd have to get inside it. That was easy. Two doors stood ajar and he slipped through one entrance and squatted under a table. It didn't take him long to realize that there was no white cat in the bar. Curiously, however, there were images of white cats all over the place. On the walls, behind the bar, pictures and photographs of white cats were used as decoration. None of these looked in the least like Pinkie.

Now Sammy was faced with a problem. Yes, it was easy to get inside one part of the building. But how to explore the rest of it? It was pointless to call for her here. The din in this room would drown any sound he could make. He withdrew slowly from the shelter of the table, taking care to avoid clumsy human feet.

'Hello, who's this?' cried a man sitting at the table, who bent down to give Sammy a stroke or two. 'Haven't seen you before. Oh! What's the matter?' Sammy had flinched as the man's coarse hands brushed his sore sides. 'Martha!' the man called loudly to the landlady. 'Here's a funny thing. There seems to be another injured cat in your pub.'

'Where?' The woman came in front of the bar. 'That tabby? He looks all right to me. Where's he injured, then?'

'He didn't like being touched,' the man replied. 'Looked as though it pained him.'

The landlady bent down. Sammy sensed he was in no danger and stayed still. But he flinched again when she began to feel his body. 'Must be bruised or something,' she said. 'Donald's in the other bar. He might have a look at him.' She carefully picked Sammy up and carried him through to the self-same room in which Pinkie had been installed. Then, leaving the door open, she went to fetch the vet. Sammy took the opportunity to run out

of the room and up the stairs. He had distinctly smelt
Pinkie's scent in the room and was convinced he would
soon find her. But, though he called persistently for her,
there was no answering miaow and in all the rooms he
was able to explore he found nothing.

He wasn't permitted much time on his own. Martha
soon located him and, half amused by Sammy's cheek,
but half scolding too, she carried him down to the vet.

'I don't think there's much wrong,' Donald said after
giving Sammy a quick look-over. 'Probably just a bruise
or two as you thought. But I'll be able to tell better if I
can get him to the surgery. I could take him back with
me if that's all right?'

'Do what you like, Donald. He's not my cat,' replied
the landlady.

'No. You don't know where he comes from?'

'Not anywhere down our road, anyway,' she stated.
'I know all the cats around here. It's odd how these
strange visitors keep turning up on my premises. I told
you about the last one. She was definitely a stray. But this
one is *someone's* pet, I'll be bound. He's a fine specimen,
isn't he?'

'He is indeed. His owners have been feeding him
well.'

Sammy was carted off to the veterinary surgery where
Monty was already a patient. The black cat had been put
on a high-nutrition diet which the vet was sure would
restore him to full health in a few days.

The tabby underwent a more through examination
and was then bundled into a pen next to Monty. The
vet made quite sure Sammy had everything he needed
for the next few hours and then closed up the surgery.

Monty stared at Sammy resentfully. 'I don't believe

this,' he growled. 'You seem to shadow me wherever I go.'

'Don't blame me,' Sammy retorted. 'I didn't ask to come here and be caged up. What's the point of it all?'

'Presumably you're in some kind of distress?' Monty queried. 'I've been here before with my owners, when I had an injured foot. The man did something to it which made it better, but I wasn't kept in this place. The girl brought me here this time. I wish my owners would come and collect me.'

Sammy explained the circumstances which had led up to his confinement.

'The man must have thought there was something wrong with you,' Monty deduced. 'You'll be looked after until you're better.'

'There's nothing wrong with me and I don't want to be looked after,' Sammy asserted. 'I must find my mate. She's been taken off somewhere else by the humans and –'

'Your mate? Huh!' Monty scoffed. 'Your interest in her has suddenly been reawakened now she's disappeared! When she was around you didn't want anything to do with her.'

'I've been very much at fault,' Sammy admitted remorsefully. 'I don't know what happened to me. I ... I ...'

'I know all right,' Monty stated emphatically. 'You forgot everything else in your greed for my food. Well, you can't get at it here! There's no convenient little door this time for you to slip through and pinch it all.'

'Oh, I don't want your food,' Sammy replied. 'Look, I've got some of my own. I just want to get out of here and begin my search.'

'How will you know where to go?'

'I must first consult with the fox who told me about Pinkie's capture. He mentioned one of his own kind that had been tended by humans. Maybe those humans are looking after Pinkie.'

'Quite likely. She's a stray – not dissimilar to a wild creature. They don't have strays in here. Animals are always brought in by their owners. You're the exception, of course! But does the fox know where you should go?'

'I don't know,' Sammy replied glumly. 'I can only ask. But I can't do anything while I'm shut up here. And, though I hate to be called it, I *am* a stray.'

'You *were*. Now you could pass for a pet like me. Any human would be fooled, including the man here. So even though there's nothing wrong with you, you'll be kept in this place. The man will expect you to be claimed by owners.'

—18—

A stray again

There was nothing Sammy could do about it. His mythi-
cal owners were awaited. Notices were displayed in the
surgery waiting-room and in the bars of the White Cat
concerning the identity of the unknown tabby but they
didn't produce any information. No one knew who he
was. Two days after Sammy had been taken by the vet,
the girl who fed Monty came to collect her charge.
Monty was perfectly fit again and his owners would
soon be home. The girl happened to notice Sammy.

'Oh, you've got him here, have you? Is he unwell?'

'No, he's all right really. We're trying to trace his
owners. Do you know him, then?'

'I found him in the Collins's living-room,' the girl
explained. 'He's the cat who was probably stealing
Monty's food.'

'Well! So he's the culprit. Where does he come
from?'

'I don't know,' the girl replied. 'And if no one else
does, it begins to look as if he doesn't have a home,
doesn't it?'

'That's not likely,' was the vet's opinion. 'He's too
well cared for.'

'He's quite a handsome cat,' the girl said. 'I wouldn't
mind having him myself if nobody else comes forward.'

'Really? Are you serious, Carol? It would help me out, you know. I can't keep him here indefinitely.'

'Then it's settled, Mr Fairhurst. If no one's claimed him by the time Mr and Mrs Collins are back to take care of Monty, *I'll* give him a home.'

By the end of that week, Monty was reunited with his master and mistress. Carol told them what the vet had said and done for him and also about Sammy whom she was about to adopt. 'I think he must have a big appetite,' she joked. 'He wanted to eat Monty's meal as well as his own.'

'But if no one's missed him, maybe no one was feeding him,' Mrs Collins said. 'He was probably very hungry.'

Carol was excited by the prospect of her new pet. But Sammy, who had so well acted the part, had no wish to be one in reality. He waited for the first opportunity to escape. And it wasn't long in coming.

Carol had no proper carrying basket of her own. She took a stout zip-up holdall to the vet's to carry Sammy in. They got him in all right, zipped up the bag and left a small gap for Sammy's head. Everything went to plan until the girl got to her front door and put the bag down to look for her key. Sammy's strength had been sadly underestimated. A long period of the very best food had done wonders for him. He saw his chance and exerted himself to widen the gap and squeeze through. The zip was forced back and Sammy burst into the open, scrambled clear and was off down the road almost before Carol had realized what had happened.

At first Sammy wasn't sure of the way to go. He soon discovered, however, that this road led to the church and then he recognized his surroundings. Before long he was back on the towpath, running towards the fox's den.

There had been a lengthy wet period and the vegetation everywhere was saturated. The river had risen and driftwood littered the bank. The fox's den, washed clean by the river water, held no trace of its fine-weather occupant. Sammy glanced about for the unfortunate animal. He wandered into the barren field where Pinkie had caught a rabbit. On a hummock of muddy matted grass lay the prone body of the ancient fox. Sammy approached nervously. There were no signs of life.

'Fox! Can you hear me?' Sammy whispered.

Abruptly the fox wriggled upright and stood on shaky legs. 'Oh. It's you. I was playing dead, just to be on the safe side.'

'Very convincing too,' Sammy commented.

'Didn't you bring a rabbit then?' the fox asked with disappointment. 'I thought, after all this time, you must have found one.'

'Rabbit?' Sammy queried. 'No, I'm looking for a white cat.' Then, all at once, he remembered. 'I'm sorry, I'm afraid I forgot all about your request. But I haven't seen any rabbits anyway.'

'I tried to catch one here,' the fox said gloomily. 'Of course it was far too quick for me. I only succeeded in exhausting myself. I've hardly enough strength to catch a worm.'

'Perhaps I can do something about that,' Sammy offered.

'That's not why you came all the way back here, is it?' the fox said. 'You want something from me.'

'Yes. That's true,' Sammy admitted. 'I need your guidance if you can give it me. It's about the little white cat. We spoke before and . . . Goodness! What's that?'

A train was approaching the bridge. It began to rumble across. Sammy cowered close to the muddy ground. The noise was unbearable, far worse than all the traffic noise he had ever heard in London. Eventually the train rattled away into the distance.

'How often does that happen?' Sammy gasped.

'Now and again. You get used to it.'

Sammy shuddered. 'I don't think I'd live long enough,' he said. 'But now it's quieter, let me ask you: the fox who was injured and made well by the humans. Where was he taken to?'

'They have a place, it seems, where they care for animals like him.'

'Yes, and I think my mate has been taken there!'

'The white cat?'

'Yes, Pinkie. But where *is* the place?'

The fox sighed. He was tired, wet and hungry as usual. He wasn't up to Sammy's eager questioning. 'All I know is,' he said wearily, 'that it's on the other side of the river. The fox could tell he was crossing the water.'

Sammy's heart sank. It sounded hopeless and he didn't want to accept the information. 'How could he be sure?' he demanded, almost accusingly.

'He must have been in a boat,' the fox answered patiently. 'I suppose he was carried across in that way. I can't tell you any more.'

'All right,' Sammy mumbled. 'Thank you, anyway. So I'm beaten before I start. I hoped to find her. But now –'

'There's another way of crossing the river,' the fox told him. 'By that bridge. People walk over it, so why can't you?'

'What, there? Where that monstrous machine came? I couldn't go there!' Sammy cried. The idea alone terrified him.

'You'd have to go by night, of course,' the fox explained. 'It's always quiet then. But – well, it's up to you, isn't it?' He began to limp away. He'd had more than enough of this discussion which was of no importance to *him*.

Sammy saw that he must face crossing the bridge if he were to have even the remotest chance of finding Pinkie. 'I'll do it!' he vowed to himself. 'As soon as it's dark.' But he wasn't ready just yet to go it alone. He trotted after the fox. 'I – I don't suppose you'd care to accompany me?'

The fox turned and stared disbelievingly. 'What a novel idea,' he said. It was a long time since any creature had courted his company. 'I appreciate the invitation. But, as you can see, I'd be a liability.'

'Oh no, I don't think so,' said Sammy. 'Once we've eaten that rabbit together, you'll be ready for anything.'

'You mean you can catch one?' The fox's tired old eyes flickered briefly with life and his threadbare tail began to swish. 'This isn't a joke, is it?'

'You watch me!' Sammy cried.

'I will, you can count on it. Go to that stream. That's where you're most likely to see them.'

Undisturbed by humans, who seldom passed such a bleak spot, Sammy turned hunter once more. In his younger days he had been a very successful rabbit hunter and, as he lay in wait by the stream, he recalled his early life with Pinkie in Quartermile Field. The old fox, well to the rear, licked his chops in anticipation. Death from starvation had stared him in the face more than once. Now the help he had so often longed for had been offered without his even asking for it.

Sammy's skill hadn't deserted him. Just as Pinkie had

done, he found a rabbit on the open stretch of ground. The prey, for so long secure from predators, was too bold and Sammy didn't need more than an even chance. He pounced and killed an old rabbit who had survived far longer than most of his kind in the wild. The fox was so ravenous he wanted to eat it at once.

'Hadn't we better take it to your den?' Sammy suggested.

'It's cold and wet in there. I've been flooded out again.'

Sammy had spied a human figure on the other side of the bridge. 'Better wet and cold than interrupted,' he advised.

'Oh, come on then,' muttered the fox, who was drooling so much he could hardly talk.

Carefully, and with considerable effort, Sammy hauled the carcass to the hole in the bank. It was just as well he did so because the lone figure was the girl Carol who had been searching for him ever since he escaped from her bag.

'Quickly, get in, Fox,' he snapped at the stumbling animal in his anxiety.

The fox crept into his slimy lair and Sammy followed, pulling the rabbit in after him. They were only just in time. Footsteps crunched nearby on the gravelly towpath. The animals didn't move a muscle. Then the fox could hold out no longer. He snatched at the kill and tore at its pelt. His stomach rumbled sympathetically. Sammy let the fox eat the lion's share of the meat. He shivered in the dank, smelly earth. But he was hidden and he was free.

When the fox had eaten his fill, breathed a satisfied sigh and fallen asleep, Sammy thought about Pinkie. What would happen when she was well again? Would the humans release her as they had the injured fox? If so, he would never find her. Hunched against the cold Sammy murmured, 'Pooh, Foxy, you're not the best perfumed of friends.' He waited impatiently for dusk.

Pinkie lay in her darkened shelter, listening to other cat voices. She was feeling lonely. That morning her immediate neighbour, a black cat like Monty, had been taken away by some young humans. Later, his pen was filled by a newcomer, a tortoiseshell. The new cat, like herself, had been brought in injured. It had stayed quiet all day, either asleep or too weak to talk. Pinkie wanted company. She prowled around her pen.

'Are you awake?' she asked her neighbour. 'Are you awake yet?'

'Yes,' came a faint reply.

Pinkie came to a halt and pressed her face to the side of her cage. 'Are you in pain?'

'Yes.'

'Were you caught by a patrol?'

'What's that?'

'You know – those humans who round up strays.'

'I never heard of anything like that. I was injured by some cruel boys. They threw stones at me.'

'How horrible!' Pinkie exclaimed. 'Are you badly hurt?'

'I think so. I was rescued by an adult human who brought me here.'

'Are you someone's pet?'

'Not me,' said the strange cat. 'I lived wild.'

'So did I,' said Pinkie. 'Have you never heard the tramping feet?'

'I don't know what you mean. There's nothing like that round here.'

'But I've heard them,' Pinkie insisted. 'Soon after my mate and I reached this area.'

'You must have heard something else,' the tortoise-shell said. 'I can assure you, if there were anything like patrols or round-ups in my neck of the woods, I would know all about it.'

Pinkie's thoughts raced. *Could* they have been mis-taken? Could Sammy's plan and their separation have been unnecessary all along? If so, what an awful irony that she had ended up in this place, while he was – well, where was he? Still hiding in another cat's home?

The tortoiseshell sighed.

'I'm sorry if I've tired you,' Pinkie said.

'It's all right. I'll sleep again in a bit. So you had a mate?'

'Yes. Sammy – a tabby. But what are you called?'

'The other cats know me as Shelley. And you?'

'Pinkie.'

Shelley was amused. 'Why – do you have pink fur? But tell me about how you lost your mate. Did he die? How did you come here?'

Pinkie said, 'No, he didn't die. But he changed so much he became like a stranger. There's a lot to tell and I don't want to weary you.'

'I'd like to hear,' Shelley said. 'After all, there's not much else to do, is there?'

So Pinkie related all the events, from the flight from the park to the day she'd been brought here and put in the pen. And while she was telling her story, Sammy was doing his best to wake the slumbering fox. It was night and he was impatient to be off.

19

Across the bridge

The old fox took a lot of waking. His unusually full stomach had sent him into a heavy sleep. Sammy's efforts to rouse him became quite violent and the tabby ended by giving the fox's tatty brush a sharp nip.

'Oh! Oh!' the fox grunted. 'What's that? Yes, I see you. You're still here then?'

'Of course I'm still here,' Sammy hissed angrily. 'We're going together, aren't we?'

'Going where? I'm only half awake.'

'Well, make yourself fully awake,' Sammy growled. 'We've got to cross the bridge.'

'Oh, the bridge. Yes.' The fox got to his feet. 'Good. It's dark.' He stretched and looked out at the river. 'I must have been dreaming,' he muttered. 'I thought I'd been washed out and was floating away on the water.'

'Never mind all that,' said Sammy. 'Let's get going.'

'Right. Mustn't keep the rabbit-hunter waiting,' the fox replied, chuckling to himself. He led Sammy to a flight of narrow steps which they had to climb to get on to the bridge. 'Up here,' he indicated.

There was some difficulty in getting to the top. Whereas Sammy sprinted up eagerly, the other animal's age and infirmity were against him, and when he reached the footway the fox hung his head, gasping for breath.

'This isn't a good start,' Sammy declared. 'If you've
worn yourself out already, how are we going to get on?
Perhaps I'd better continue alone.'

'No. No – don't do that,' the fox panted. He wasn't
used to companionship and he was beginning to enjoy
it. 'I'll try not to hold you up. Another couple of' – gasp
– 'meals like the last one' – gasp – 'and I'll be as fit as
you are.'

'Very well,' said Sammy. 'But don't count on rabbits wherever we go. Now, come on, let's get across
before one of those monsters drives us back down
again.'

On the other side of the river another flight of
steps took them down to a road. 'Which way now?'
Sammy asked.

'How should I know?' the fox replied. 'I've never been
here before either.'

They looked up at some tall buildings fronting the
riverside. Next to these was an open space occupied
by machinery and building materials. Sammy had an
inkling that this couldn't be the sort of place he was
looking for. 'Let's go the other way,' he suggested.

The road ran alongside the river. It was quiet. They
passed an occasional house. 'If we find the boat,' said
the fox, 'it may give you a clue.'

'Boat? What boat?' Sammy queried, puzzled.

'The one that brought your white cat, like the fox,
across the water.'

'No. Oh no,' Sammy replied. 'Pinkie wouldn't have
been carried by boat.' He knew enough about human
behaviour and motor traffic to discount the idea.

Now the fox looked mystified. 'How else could she
have crossed the river? Does she fly?' It was evident
that he didn't understand much about vehicles and
roads.

'There must be another bridge,' Sammy said confidently. 'And when we find it, we'll be on our way.'

'Another bridge? *I've* never seen one,' the fox grunted. He paused to lap at a puddle by the kerbside.

Sammy waited for him. 'If you need a rest, just say so,' he invited his companion. 'Your legs aren't as young as mine.'

'Huh! No. I sometimes feel I never was young,' the ancient beast remarked. 'But I'm game for a few more paces if I don't expire first.'

'You're a droll one,' Sammy said. 'Just how old are you?'

'I'm as old as my limbs and older than my teeth,' the fox answered jocularly.

Some trees grew along the river bank and, after a while, the fox's breathing became so hoarse that Sammy flopped down under some alders to give him time to recover.

'Thank you,' said the aged creature with an appreciative wag of his tail, and collapsed beside him. 'This is a nice spot. I might find a better place for my den on this side.'

'You could hardly have a worse one,' Sammy commented.

A little later they continued. Sammy's search for a second bridge was the key to his future progress. If he didn't find one, he had no way of tracing Pinkie's journey. He walked slowly for the benefit of the older animal. Eventually Sammy became tired himself, and together they looked for good shelter where they could have a proper sleep.

'Daylight isn't far away,' the fox wheezed. 'We have to take care.'

And then they saw it – or at least Sammy did. A stone

bridge spanned the river ahead as they rounded a bend, and the lights of a car illuminated its length as it crossed from right to left.

'I knew it!' Sammy exclaimed. 'This is wonderful. Now I have something to go on. There will be a road leading from the bridge end and that's the way I take.'

'Well, it will be without me,' the fox told him, 'if you're going in daylight. I can't be seen wandering along human byways. I'm vermin to them.'

'No question of it,' Sammy said at once. 'It's just as risky for me, only from another aspect. Can you make it to the bridge?'

'Keep going,' croaked the fox. 'I think I must be already asleep, so I probably won't notice.'

The road they were on ran up to a junction at the foot of the bridge. The two animals, of course, veered away and on to the river bank itself. As dawn broke they lay down under the arch of the bridge, close up to the stonework. It was still dark there and they felt secure enough. The fox wrapped his mangy brush around his muzzle and was soon blissfully asleep. Sammy curled up too and drifted into a doze. At every slight sound he opened his eyes, blinked, and napped again. The fox began to twitch and whimper so that Sammy guessed he was dreaming.

'Poor beast,' Sammy murmured. 'I think his life has been very hard. I wonder if he'll come with me all the way?'

Traffic noise on the bridge woke them both fully during the morning. A mallard was paddling at the water's edge. The fox slowly got to his feet and stood watching it, licking his chops.

'I can't catch that, I can't catch that,' he chanted to himself miserably. 'But I wish I could.'

Sammy rose. Keeping his head and body still and fixing his eyes on the bird, he stalked slowly towards it. Only his legs moved as he hugged the ground. A few paces, then complete stillness while the duck faced him, then a few paces more . . . The duck was dipping and splashing briskly. The fox was gripped by an unbearable excitement. He trembled like a leaf, willing himself not to dash forward and ruin their chances. Sammy was almost on his quarry when the mallard began to paddle swiftly away. The tabby hesitated. He didn't like water. The fox, made desperate by a lost opportunity, raced past him and into the river. Now the duck realized the danger it was in and flapped its wings furiously. But it was a little slow to take off and the fox lunged at it, his few teeth managing to take hold of one wing. The mallard struggled valiantly. The fox couldn't keep hold and Sammy saw he must come to his aid. He stepped into the water, shuddered, then swam out resolutely to his companion. Seizing the duck's other wing, he steadied the flapping and the two animals paddled to the bank with their prey. Sammy finished the job. His teeth gripped the bird's throat until it ceased to struggle. The animals shook the water from themselves.

'What a prize!' crowed the fox. 'I could never have brought that off by myself. I'm in your debt. But of course we'll go shares.'

Sammy didn't reply. He was conscious that his once glossy coat was completely spoilt. Soaked to the skin by dirty river water he only needed to glance at the fox's appearance to know what he himself looked like – filthy. He had disparaged Pinkie's appearance but she had never looked as awful as this. 'We need to dry out,' he said finally. How he would have enjoyed Monty's nice warm room and a soft chair to lie on.

The fox, naturally, cared nothing for looks or for the

discomfort of being thoroughly wet. He was already busy wrenching off mouthfuls of plumage from the duck's body. Some of the feathers wafted away and landed on the surface of the river, drifting downstream like a flotilla of tiny boats with curved prows.

Sammy looked around for a sunny patch of ground. He was content to let the fox deal with the preparation of the meal.

'This is good meat,' the old creature said as he tore off his first mouthful.

Sammy slumped down on the bank and made a worthy attempt to clean himself. Later he would eat too, but now he wanted to devote his thoughts to Pinkie and the next stage of his search.

The fox kept well out of sight during the rest of the day, his meagre body pressed to the cold stone under the arch of the bridge. Sammy dried his fur and wandered here and there, only joining the fox in the late afternoon to share his meal.

'I haven't felt so strong in an age,' the ancient beast remarked. 'The food's put new heart into me. What do we do next?'

'When it's quite dark we'll follow the road from the bridge. It could be very hazardous. And you're not used to traffic, are you?'

'No, I don't seek out such things,' the fox replied cheerily, 'but if we have to meet it, I'll be ready.'

'No, no, we don't meet it, we *mustn't* meet it, 'Sammy corrected him. 'We avoid it at all costs. Otherwise –'

'We're dead, eh?' the fox chipped in. 'I get it. Well, I'll be behind you, so you'll see it first!'

Sammy was impatient for dusk. When at last he was satisfied it was quiet enough to proceed, he set off up the bank. The fox, who had spent most of his life short of food, grabbed the remnants of the mallard which he intended to carry along with him. There would be no waste; he would see to that.

The road was easy to find. There was no pavement. Shrubby plants and the occasional tree grew on either side. Hugging the extreme edge of the road, so that their sides brushed the vegetation, the two animals went forward with extreme wariness. There were no buildings of any kind. The road was quiet for a long time. Then, in the distance, they could see the brilliant light from a car's headlamps. Sammy calmly made tracks into the thick vegetation. The fox followed him and they simply waited until the road was clear again. Thus they made their way along.

The half-eaten duck carcass was proving to be a burden. The fox's jaws ached badly with the effort of lugging it around. Every so often he dropped it to give himself a rest and also to try a different grip. He had dropped it for the umpteenth time when Sammy glimpsed the approach of another vehicle. At this point along the road there was an almost impenetrable tangle of bramble and other plants which offered no immediate sanctuary. Sammy ran on quickly to look for a gap.

'Here, Fox! Run!' he called as soon as he found one, diving into the foliage himself.

The fox snatched up his prey, juggled with it to get a better hold, and started forward. But, unfamiliar as he was with the startling speed of a motor vehicle, he had lost too much time. The blinding light of the headlamps dazzled him and he lurched sideways. Sammy saw that the fox had put himself in peril. He burrowed through the thickly massed stems, clamped his teeth on the fox's brush and yanked him backwards with all his might. It wasn't forceful enough a pull to get the bewildered animal quite clear of the road, but just enough to allow

a hair's breadth of space between him and the car as
it sped past. The yank on his tail made the fox squeal
with pain so that he dropped the mallard again. It was
promptly squashed by the car's rear wheel.

Stunned and shocked, the fox stumbled into shelter.
'I . . . I . . .' he stammered and couldn't find words to
express his feelings.

'Just in the nick of time. You were lucky,' Sammy
said.

The fox gulped repeatedly. 'I – I – I was,' he stuttered.
'Lucky to have you. To – to – bother about me. No
one has taken such care of me before. But why?' He
was puzzled. He had all but forgotten the impulses of
friendship.

'Well – because I like you,' Sammy answered easily,
'and so I don't want to see you killed.'

The fox gulped again and gaped. He had no more
words.

'Are you ready to move on?' Sammy prompted.

'Er – yes,' the fox murmured.

'We've lost our next meal,' the tabby pointed out.
'Look at it. There's not a mouthful to be had now.'

The fox seemed to recover himself. 'Carried it all
that way for nothing,' he muttered, 'and never got a
bite out of it.'

'We had the best of it earlier,' Sammy said philosophi-
cally. 'We'll catch something else.'

The fox glared at the flattened carcass as if trying to
assess whether he could even now salvage part of it.

'Come on, Fox,' Sammy said brightly. 'Don't waste
time over that. It nearly killed you.'

The old creature sighed, then obediently followed.
'You saved my life,' he suddenly said in a half-whisper.
'You saved me.' There was still a tone of wonder in
his voice. He simply couldn't get used to the idea.

'Sammy saved my life.' He was speaking to himself now, as though he needed to repeat it again in order to grasp it.

'So! You remember my name,' Sammy cried. 'You've never used it before.'

'From now on,' said the fox, 'I shall use it all the time. No one has bothered about me for such a long time. But you . . . well! And an old fool like me!'

Sammy was pleased with himself. He was genuinely glad that the fox had survived and especially that he had been able to rescue him. 'I hope when we find Pinkie you'll stay with us,' he said.

The fox thought about it. 'I'd like to,' he said. 'But when you're together again you won't want me around. I'd only be a nuisance, taking food from your mouths. *I* can't hunt any more.'

'Really? I seem to remember you were the one who caught the duck in the first instance,' Sammy reminded him.

'Well! So I was,' the fox replied in astonishment. 'Perhaps I'm not so useless after all.'

20

'Where have you come from?'

The first building came into view around a bend in the road. It was all in darkness. Could this be the place? There was an open entrance from the road with a garden surrounding it. Sammy and the fox entered the grounds side by side.

'I don't think there are animals here,' said Sammy. 'There isn't a sound.'

'Wait here,' the fox said. 'Let my nose be the judge. I may be on my last legs, but my sense of smell hasn't deserted me.' He scouted around the building, muzzle to the ground. He soon returned. 'You're quite right,' he announced. 'Only human scents here.'

It was the same story with the next two houses. Sammy was beginning to feel disheartened when they came across a quite different style of building. This one was well set back from the road and was in the form of a large cube. Several of its many windows were illuminated. There was a wide parking area to the front and the sides. Already from a distance away, Sammy's sharp ears picked up animal sounds. He became very excited. The fox, however, began to look nervous.

'This must be it!' Sammy exclaimed. 'Two . . . three times I heard a dog. Different noises; different animals. So there's a number of them here. I haven't yet heard a cat.'

'Go closer,' the fox said. 'I'll stay here in the shadows.'

'I was hoping you'd use your nose again,' Sammy said.

'Oh, I can smell cat from here.' The fox sounded quite sure about it. 'There are many scents: all kinds of creatures.'

'Pinkie will be here, then,' Sammy said. 'There can't be two places like this.'

'What will you do now?' the fox asked.

'I'll see if there's a way in. If not, I must wait around until a door or a window is opened.'

'Supposing it's daylight by then?'

'Makes no difference,' Sammy replied. 'I have to get inside to find Pinkie.'

The fox looked uncertain about it. 'I suppose this is where we part for the present, then,' he said unhappily. 'I can't risk being around here in daylight. If you find your mate, what are your plans?'

'To get her away from here. But it may not be possible.'

'What if it isn't?'

'I don't know,' Sammy admitted. 'I haven't thought that far ahead. Look, Fox, don't leave just yet. It's an awfully long way back. Perhaps you might find that better den somewhere around here, away from the river. Let me go and take a look around. You're safe for the present. I'll come back shortly and tell you what I've discovered.'

The fox was pleased with this idea. 'All right, Sammy,' he said brightly.

Sammy went off resolutely, leaving the fox to seek a more secluded spot. There was a fence all around the area. In one corner a stand of hazel sprouted, and here the fox lay down on the residue of last winter's leaves. Sammy, meanwhile, prowled the length of the building, staying close to the wall. Nothing open there. Round the back next, and there *was* a window open. Sammy looked at it intently, pondering his chances of jumping to the opening. He thought he could probably make it. Anyway it was worth trying. He quickly trotted back to inform his friend.

Sammy's calls, audible inside the building, set two dogs barking. The fox came, wagging his tail.

'I've found a way in,' Sammy told him. 'I'm going to give it a try. Will you wait for me?'

The fox looked nervous. He licked his lips anxiously. 'Yes, for a while. But I'll have to move before daybreak.'

'Very well. If you don't see me – or *both* of us – before then, where will you be?' Sammy turned, eager to go.

'Back in the undergrowth,' the fox answered. 'You know – where you saved me. I'll stay hidden. Will you come for me?'

'Of course I will.'

'All right. Be careful, Sammy. And good luck!'

'The same to you.' Sammy returned to the rear of the building. Balancing himself for a leap, he sprang upwards and managed to grapple a hold on the window frame. He teetered there for a bit, his eyes peering into the darkness inside for a clue as to what was before him. A dog started to yap. It sounded close by. Sammy's fur rose along his back and his body swayed. Was he going to jump down into a dog's jaws? Moments later, his eyes could make out a room with two rows of pens stretching away along either wall. He could smell dog – warm bodies and coats – plainly. But there were no animals running loose.

'Here goes,' he murmured to himself, pressing his front paws against the inside wall in preparation for the leap down. He sprang, and landed without difficulty. More dogs, roused by Sammy's soft thud, began to bark. Now he could see some of them, peeping through the bars of their pens and suspicious of any strange noise. He had to run the gauntlet of their eager eyes and tongues if he were to begin his search. It was a daunting prospect. Sammy reminded himself that the dogs were all safely out of reach and, plucking up courage, slunk forwards.

'Who's this?' 'What are you doing?' 'How did you get here?' 'We're sick, don't disturb us!' 'Keep away!' 'This is my cage!' 'Who are you?' the dogs yapped and barked as they saw or scented Sammy. Not all of them were angry or indignant; some merely curious or inquisitive, others too ill to bother at all. Sammy thought he could make use of the inquisitive kind. He hastened to get some information before the din came inevitably to human attention.

'Are there cats here?' he asked a Jack Russell boldly.

'Sure there are. Why shouldn't there be?'

'Where? Where are they?' Sammy hissed urgently.

'I don't know. Further along, maybe. Or in the outside area where the fit dogs are.'

Sammy continued quickly onward. He had no idea what he would do if he suddenly came across Pinkie in one of these cages. Soon he caught the distinct smell of a male cat. He went straight towards the source: around a corner and along a short corridor to more, but smaller, pens in two tiers.

A large tabby was in the first one. It was bigger even

than Sammy and was crouching in its pen, its ears pricked against the diminishing barks. It saw Sammy and cried out in amazement, 'I wondered what had set them off. Who are you? How did you get out?'

Sammy replied, 'I'm Sammy and I've got *in*! Through the window. Phew, it's hot in here.'

The other tabby blinked and looked at him incredulously. 'Are you a mad cat?' it demanded. 'Where have you come from?'

'Outside,' Sammy answered simply. 'I'm looking for my mate – a little white cat.'

'Very likely!' the tabby spat. 'Well, you won't find a mate here. They're all shut away. You must have taken leave of your senses.'

Sammy tried to explain. 'We were separated. Pinkie got injured and I think the humans brought her here.'

'They certainly didn't,' growled the other. 'There are no pink cats here. Whoever heard of such a thing?'

'No, no, a *white* cat. Pink tongue, pink ears. *They* gave her her name. Have you seen a little white female in here? With blue eyes? Quickly! I'm sure someone will be coming.'

'I can only see what I can see from this enclosure,' the tabby replied sourly. 'And all I can see is a black cat, a tabby like you, a black-and-white and a tortoiseshell. So you're out of luck!'

'Not if there are others you *can't* see!' Sammy snapped. 'Has confinement made you objectionable or were you always like this?'

'Stay here much longer and you'll find out!'

Sammy walked on purposefully, past the black cat and the tabby, past the black-and-white, all of whom started to dart questions at him, and stopped by the tortoiseshell. She was bandaged and asleep. Ignoring all the demands and enquiries, he moved on again.

Next to the tortoiseshell was a little white cat with blue eyes. Pinkie said, 'I thought it was you.'

Sammy was ecstatic. He pushed his face against the wire so that his whiskers brushed hers. 'Pinkie!' he whispered tenderly. 'How did you know?'

'I heard your voice, of course. I thought you would come. Have you ceased to be a pet?'

'Yes. I'm Sammy the vagabond again.'

'*My* Sammy?'

'Yes.'

'How did you find me?'

There was a lot to explain and talk about, on both sides. But now wasn't the time. 'The old fox put me on your trail,' said Sammy. 'He's outside now. Is there any way out of your cage?'

'Of course not!' Pinkie replied. 'D'you think I'd still be in it if there were?'

'Then you're not hurt?'

'I was, but that was a while ago. It wasn't anything much, Sammy. What are we going to do?'

'I don't know. I need to think about this. When will your cage be opened?'

'When I'm fed. And sometimes the humans have to clean up. Then I'm taken out and –' She stopped suddenly. There was the noise of footsteps. 'Somebody's coming,' Pinkie hissed. 'You must go!'

'No, no,' Sammy pleaded. 'I've only just found you. I'll hide.'

'There's nowhere to hide,' she wailed. 'Oh, footsteps, footsteps ... we've feared them in one way or another for so long. Sammy, you must run. Please! Don't get yourself captured too. Stay free or we'll always be apart.'

Sammy saw the sense in her words. But he was overcome by sadness. To have found Pinkie against all the odds and then, almost at once, be forced to abandon her again!

'I'll be back,' he whispered with determination. 'Good-bye for now.' He ran between the rows of cages, round the corner and up to the window. The footsteps pursued him. Light flooded the rooms as a young woman arrived to investigate the commotion. Sammy's thick tail was illuminated as he disappeared through the window. He was gone in a flash. The woman stood looking at the open window and doubted that she had really seen what she thought she had seen.

Sammy, sick at heart, sought out the fox and told him what he had discovered.

'You found her!' the fox exclaimed, wagging his tail vigorously. He was almost as excited as Sammy had been.

'Yes. I found her only to leave her once more. I must go back.' Sammy prowled about, unable to keep still.

'Wait. You can't go back now. Daylight's coming soon,' the fox counselled him. 'And what could you do, anyway?'

'Nothing,' Sammy answered hoarsely. 'Oh, Fox, help me. Can you think of a plan?'

'Maybe. Come, Sammy. We must leave here and find somewhere more secure.' Now the fox led the way, with Sammy following, full of frustration. Further along the road a clump of woodland offered protection. The fox and the cat ran underneath the trees and were embraced by deep shadows.

'This is marvellous,' said the fox, who felt at home at once. He sprawled at the foot of a huge oak with branches that blotted out the fading moonlight. Sammy squatted next to him, still on edge.

'Sammy, you don't need to go back into that place of humans,' the fox said slowly.

'Of course I do,' Sammy argued. 'What do you mean?'

'You said that Pinkie had recovered from her hurt. So the humans made her well again.'

'Yes, I suppose so.'

'Well then, they'll soon release her. Do you remember what I told you about the injured fox?'

'Yes. And so you think they won't keep Pinkie?'

'Why should they if she's well? All you have to do is to stay nearby – around here perhaps; it's a suitable spot – and soon you'll be able to rejoin her without putting yourself at risk.'

'But Pinkie won't know that,' Sammy demurred. 'She won't know where I am. I have to go back to explain.'

'Not now,' the fox insisted. 'You'd be caught for sure. Aren't you tired after all this activity? Why don't you sleep through the daytime and go back after dusk? *I* couldn't walk another step. I don't know how I've kept up with you.'

'I'll try to curb my impatience,' Sammy replied. 'I know you're right.'

'Good. We'll be quite safe here. We couldn't have found a better place. Later I'll nose around a bit. Talk to the locals. There might just be room for a mangy old fox to make himself a den.'

— 21 —

At the sign of the White Cat

The fox was right about Pinkie in one respect. Now she had made a full recovery, there was no intention of keeping her any longer than it took to find her a home. The only way she would be released was into the care of some loving humans. However, it just so happened that there were some people who were interested in her.

The landlord of the White Cat and his wife Martha had lost not only their pet in Snowy, but their mascot as well. Snowy had been the living symbol of the pub and now they were without one. Martha had all along kept the picture of Pinkie in her mind. It had seemed such a strange coincidence that Pinkie had appeared on the scene requiring attention almost at the moment that their own dear white cat had been so shockingly killed. At the time the horror of Snowy's death had been so great that Martha hadn't recognized the full significance of the event. Now it appeared to her that Pinkie had somehow been sent as a replacement. The more she pondered it the more she was convinced that Pinkie was meant for the pub, and she spoke to her husband to see what he thought.

'Where is the cat now?' he asked.

'Probably still at the animal home, Bernard. Unless someone else liked the look of her.'

Bernard pursed his lips. He was wiping the bar down in preparation for morning business. He looked meditatively at Snowy's photos and the other pictures of white cats on the walls. Nothing had been changed since Snowy had gone. 'Yes, it would be nice to have a cat again,' he said. 'Give some meaning to all this. But wasn't she a stray, that one?'

'Must have been,' said Martha. 'But that doesn't matter. She'd soon settle down. She was all right with me when we had her here overnight. She seemed to like me.'

Bernard smiled. 'You have a way with you,' he acknowledged. 'All right, my dear. Why don't you give the people a ring to see if she's still there?'

Sammy could hardly contain himself during the day. He dozed for a while but spent most of the time exploring the immediate area. There were shrews and mice to be had. He caught some quite easily and left them for the old fox. The taste of Monty's meat was still too strong in his memory for Sammy to relish such skin and bone.

As the sun dipped Sammy set off for the animal home. The fox had woken and prepared to follow, but first he gulped down the rodents without bothering to give them an introduction to his few remaining teeth. The woodland pulled strongly at the fox. He wanted nothing better than to stay under its canopy and seek out a hole excavated by another creature which could serve him as a convenient den. But he knew he had to remain with Sammy until the tabby had been back inside the building. He shadowed Sammy, who for the moment had forgotten all about him.

As he neared the building Sammy increased his pace.

Dusk was falling. The main entrance door was open and a car parked near it. Sammy wondered if he dare go through that door, rather than trust to the same open window as before. He could hear voices close to the entrance. A cat was miaowing nervously. Sammy recognized Pinkie's call at once. Instinctively he miaowed back and began to run towards the open door. The fox saw him go and barked a warning as he slunk out of sight. Sammy was oblivious. All he could hear were Pinkie's increasingly anxious calls. The next moment Martha, the pub landlady, walked briskly out of the door carrying a cat basket. The cat inside was Pinkie. She called constantly, 'Sammy, follow me. Find the place we first came to.'

Martha got quickly into her car, placing Pinkie on the floor next to the driving seat. A member of staff from the animal home waved her off.

Sammy knew the kindly human from the pub straight away. She had tended him and fed him before the vet had carried him off. He knew exactly what he had to do. The fox joined him as soon as the humans had departed.

'Things look bad,' said the fox.

'No. Actually they're not,' Sammy replied. He was quite excited. 'Pinkie's got out of this place and I know where she's heading.'

'A prophet, are you?' the fox quipped.

Sammy explained about the woman. 'Pinkie will be waiting for me,' he said at last. 'So I must leave you, Fox.'

'I'll come with you, Sammy – if you like . . .'

'I would like,' said Sammy. 'But it's not the best thing for you. Why should you make the long trek back again? There's not much for you across the bridge. You wanted to make a new den. The woodland is

the place for you. No river to wash your home away
there . . .'

'No. No river,' the fox agreed. 'And no friends,' he
murmured beneath his breath so that Sammy shouldn't
hear.

'I shall know where to find you,' the tabby said
brightly. 'One day I'll bring Pinkie with me. We won't
lose each other.'

'No. Not us,' the fox vowed. But he looked glum.

'Well, I'd better make a start,' said Sammy. 'I need to
travel by night.'

'Good luck,' said the fox. 'Go carefully.'

'I will. And you also.'

Without the fox to slow him down, Sammy made good
progress, and the next morning he was once more on
the towpath. Above his head the sign of the White Cat
swung slightly in a spring breeze. So far there had been
no sign of Pinkie, however.

'Are they keeping her locked up?' Sammy mused. 'In
case she wanders off?' It was to be some time before he
found out.

Around noon about a week later the pub was as usual
beginning to bustle. It was a warm day. The doors were
open and, now fully trusted, Pinkie strolled into the
garden. She stood looking at the scene of her earlier
capture. The rabbit hutch was empty. The lop-ears had
not been replaced as Snowy had been replaced. Pinkie
expected Sammy to put in an appearance soon. She
knew he had heard her calls at the animal home and
would be seeking her. Thus the opportunity to teach
him a lesson had at last – and unexpectedly – arrived.
The tables had been turned. Now she was the pet and
Sammy the stray. It would be easy now to treat him as
he had treated her; when Monty's meat and the Church

Cat's charm had been of more importance to him than his own mate.

'I'll make him fret,' she purred. She savoured the prospect of his discomfort. 'Oh Sammy, how I've longed for such a chance!'

Sammy came into the pub garden cautiously. 'Pinkie!' he called. 'Quickly. Let's go.'

Pinkie sat perfectly still, yawned and looked away.

Sammy called again. 'Pinkie! It's me – Sammy!'

'I can see that,' she said without interest.

Sammy came close. 'You – you look well,' he said awkwardly. 'And your coat! It's spotless.'

Pinkie eyed him searchingly. 'The same can't be said of you,' she said. 'What *have* you been doing to yourself? I thought you had such high standards now?'

'But – but I told you, Pinkie. I'm not a pet any more. I'm the same Sammy you knew before. I haven't changed.'

'Oh, but you *have*,' she said, taking on the Church Cat's cultured tones. 'You were so clean, so polished, so *selfish* . . .' She fixed him with her clear blue eyes.

'Oh, I get it,' Sammy muttered. 'All right. I admit I was awful to you. Please forgive me. I don't know how it happened. The new life . . . It sort of took me over. Er – Pinkie . . .' Sammy was evidently embarrassed. 'Is there food here?'

'Of *course* there's food. I have to live. The woman's very good to me. The most succulent meat, the most –'

'Yes, all right!' Sammy cried. He licked his chops. 'Could you . . . you know, spare a little?'

'Sorry. I ate every bit,' Pinkie replied. She was really enjoying herself. 'There's only enough for one, you see.'

'Yes, I suppose there is,' Sammy said dully. 'Well, shall we go and catch a rabbit? I mean, shall *I* catch a rabbit and – and – we could share it?'

'Oh no,' said Pinkie. 'I can't do that. I live here now.' She remembered Snowy's words and repeated them. 'You see, I'm the Pub Cat.'

Sammy was dumbfounded. For a moment he couldn't find his voice. Then he mumbled, 'But you surely don't intend to stay? We're not cut out to be pets, you and I. Not really. Not permanently. . .' His voice tailed off. 'Are we?' he finished lamely.

'I don't know about you,' Pinkie replied. 'But, as far as I'm concerned – yes, I can see the advantages. Humans aren't so bad, are they? Not all of them, anyway. The ones here are kind and decent. Why should I leave? I'm fed, cared for and petted. It's a new experience for me and I'm relishing it. Being completely free – as you are now,' she said archly, 'has its advantages too. But I've suffered too much as a stray to want to go back to that kind of life again now I don't have to. You'll be fine, Sammy. I know you will. You always make out somehow. And – well, we can still meet if you want to, from time to time. Hereabouts.'

Sammy couldn't believe he was hearing this. 'I don't understand,' he said unhappily. 'When I wanted you to give up your freedom to make yourself safe from the patrols you refused.'

'There *are* no patrols,' Pinkie answered. 'No round-ups. Not in these parts. I've found out all about it.'

'But I – we – *heard* the tramping, the –'

'We thought we did,' Pinkie interrupted. 'But it was something else. There's no danger here. Pet or vagabond cat, what you will, there are no alarms for us any more. And – yes, I did refuse to join you at first in Monty's house. Well, Sammy' – Pinkie looked at him pointedly – 'we should all learn from our mistakes. I certainly have.' She turned and casually, but quite deliberately, walked away from him and in through the open pub door.

Sammy started after her disconsolately. He felt thoroughly miserable. Pinkie peeped round the door frame and watched him. Eventually he left and made his slow way to the riverside. She really felt for him. She knew only too well how miserable he would be feeling. With a sore heart but with determination none the less she said to herself, 'Sammy will soon learn. I won't punish him for ever.'

A lesson learnt

For a couple of days Sammy skulked around the tow-path. He didn't go anywhere near the White Cat, nor did he enter any of the gardens of the neighbourhood houses. He didn't wish to risk being spotted by Carol. He tried not to think about Pinkie. She had hurt his pride and he was sulking, but gradually his sulks gave way to indignation. How dare Pinkie treat him like this? He knew he had been at fault in the past, but he had never refused her a share of his food as she had done him.

'Pinkie needs reminding of that,' he growled to himself. And he returned to the pub garden.

Fortunately for Sammy the weather had stayed warm and dry, so he had not suffered much discomfort except in so far as his stomach was concerned. After the plentiful food he had been used to, he found it all the more difficult to adjust to his new meagre diet. And that was what was causing him the most aggravation.

'Look here, Pinkie,' he said as soon as he saw her, 'you're not behaving at all fairly. When I was in Monty's house I offered you a share of my food. Yet you don't –'

'Don't you mean Monty's food?' Pinkie corrected him.

'Oh, all right, Monty's. What's the difference?' Sammy

grumbled. 'The offer was there anyway. And you should do the same for me. I won't be treated like this!'

'But I can't do the same for you,' Pinkie replied sweetly. 'I don't have any of Monty's food to share with you.'

Sammy glared at her. 'So this is the way you're going to be, is it? Very well. I don't beg from *anyone*, even though I'm half starved.'

'Oh, I don't think you're starving,' Pinkie remarked lightly. 'You look healthy enough to me.'

Sammy turned away from her and stalked off. He was furious.

Of course it was no good being angry. That didn't get him anywhere. Over the next few days he came to realize just how neglected Pinkie had been whilst he was enjoying the comforts of a warm house and a full food-bowl. How lonely she must have been. He himself, without even the fox for company, felt deserted.

'I deserve all I get,' he told himself ruefully. 'What I did was shameful.' He lay against the high wall, basking in the strong sunshine and partially hidden by the long grass. A black cat sat on top of the wall, staring down at him.

'Reality caught up with you, I see,' said Monty, for it was indeed he.

The tabby glanced upwards. 'Once a vagabond always a vagabond,' he replied fatalistically. 'And who steals your food these days? The black-and-white cat?'

'Domino? Oh, no. He keeps away. My owners are back. There's no opportunity for any stranger to thieve now. And you? You don't look so plump and presentable any more. I doubt if the Church Cat would acknowledge your existence now.'

'That's no worry to me,' Sammy retorted. 'I don't want

any pet to take notice of me. I've learnt to do without all
that. What I want is for a certain little white cat to be my
companion again.'

'Then you should go and tell her so,' said Monty.

'Pinkie! Pinkie! Won't you talk to me?' Sammy sat in the
middle of the pub garden. It was late evening. The little
white cat sat under a garden table, carefully washing
her coat. She knew Sammy was there but pretended to
ignore him.

'Pinkie! I only want to talk. The way we used to. I need
your company even if it's just . . . just for a while. Won't
you talk to me?'

Pinkie looked up. 'Just for a while, then. I'm going
indoors shortly to be fed.'

Sammy swallowed but made no mention of his hunger. 'Of course. I won't interfere. I only wanted to tell
you how very much I regret the way I was before. Selfish,
greedy, cruel . . . I was all of them. And I'd do anything
for you now to make up for it. Anything. You see, I've
learnt the hard way about what you must have suffered
and I'm so miserable to think of it. I can't bear to know
you were hurt because of me.'

Pinkie began to purr quietly. But she didn't go any
closer. 'That's all over now,' she said. 'We won't talk
about it. You can come and visit me whenever you
want. But be careful. Don't lose your freedom again.
You understand me?'

'Yes. Yes, I understand. I'll take care.'

'And, Sammy – do you ever think of our kittens?'

'I never stopped thinking about them, Pinkie.'

Pinkie's purring grew louder. 'Goodbye for now,
Sammy,' she said.

'Goodbye, Pinkie.'

*   *   *

The two cats met regularly after that, mostly by night. Usually Pinkie would be waiting on the towpath under the sign of the White Cat. Sammy never asked for food but Pinkie could tell he was eating very little. One day she asked him, 'Do you ever catch a rabbit?'

'No. Not rabbit,' he answered. 'I don't like to go too far from here. I want to feel I'm close to where you are.'

Pinkie softened visibly. 'That's a kind thought,' she whispered. 'Sammy?'

'Yes?'

'Shall we see if we can catch one together?'

'D'you mean it?' Sammy cried. 'Don't you have to go back?'

'No. Not if I don't choose to,' Pinkie replied.

'Come on then, Pinkie! Race me!'

Along the dusky towpath near the railway bridge another animal had been out hunting. The pair of cats saw the beast limp away as they approached, its jaws clamped round its prey. There was no mistaking the animal's gait. 'Fox!' they both cried.

The beast turned, dropping a fat lop-eared rabbit. 'Well! Together again!' he croaked as he saw his friends and wagged his tail mightily.

'What are you doing here?' Sammy asked. 'Do you come so far to hunt?'

'No.' The fox grinned. He had lost another tooth. 'Competition over there was too tough. I couldn't cope. I need a bit of help when I want to hunt.' He grinned again and stood panting.

The cats looked at each other. 'But – the rabbit . . .' Pinkie began.

'Walked right into me,' the fox explained. 'Just like the last time. This makes a pair. It's been loose a long time.'

'Loose?' Sammy queried.

'It's not a wild rabbit,' Pinkie said. 'I know where this came from.'

'Well, do you want some?' the fox asked.

Sammy's eyes were nearly popping out of his head. 'Look at him,' said Pinkie with unmistakable affection. 'You don't have to ask!'

But Sammy said, 'It looks as though we won't need to hunt after all, Pinkie. Will you go back now?'

'Back?' she answered softly. 'What, to that boring, humdrum sort of life? When I can be prowling the river bank with you two? You bet I'm not going back! Not ever!'